Diego García Quiroga

LETTING GO
Stories of the Falklands-Malvinas War

Translated by the author from the original
Historias de los Años Sin Piel

London
*Jet*stone
2016

A *Jet*stone paperback original.

ISBN 978-1-910858-07-3

Originally published in Argentina by De Los Cuatro Vientos, Buenos Aires, as *Historias de los Años Sin Piel*.

Cover design by The Ever Shifting Subject.

CONTENTS

We are known to others but for our experience.
Our dreams are at their best an image of our hopes.

These stories describe my people and my land, and me.

They were written for my son and my two daughters.
I never had a better dream than them.

Acknowledgments

Several persons have influenced both my decision and my ability to write this book. The original impulse was born from a conversation with my older daughter, Julia. She had learned the story at school and I wanted to give her my own version.

Though writing is a lonely task, few books are written in complete solitude and this is certainly not one of them. I would therefore like to thank Bernard McGuirk, Juan García Quiroga, Mike Seear, Elena Aráoz, Jeremy Lawrance and Macdonald Daly for their unyielding encouragement and trust, as well as for their constancy and patience in suggesting, correcting and bettering my many drafts.

Most crucially, this book would have never come to be but for the loving support of my wife, Beate. She provided the energy, the stimulation and the peace of mind I needed to set in words these memories. And she always did it with a smile.

Foreword to the English edition

The stories that make up this book are my attempt to show how a part of my generation saw the world. They are centred on the most dramatic military affair that befell our country while we were young: the war against Great Britain.

At the time the war broke out Argentina was struggling to find its way back to the democracy it had enjoyed until almost forty years before, when the first of a series of *de facto* regimes took over the rule of the land. Peppered with honest but unsuccessful democratic periods, those years succeeded in widening the already significant social differences and created a distinctive aversion to authority that found its common expression in widespread mistrust towards the government, the military, the police and politicians.

This state of affairs also represented an enormous opportunity for any ideology other than democracy to penetrate and take root, a fact swiftly grasped by the international left. From late 1950s and, almost inaudibly at first but soon increasingly openly, the military and state-dependent intelligence services began to pay increasing attention to the operations and propaganda of left-wing organisations within and around the country's borders, and already in the seventies these activities had led to an dreadful internal war that – in spite of its success – further discredited the military.

This was the background against which Argentina, not finding an echo to its public insistence on the urgency to solve the issue of the islands, decided to make a show of force and help revitalize the national pride of its (by then) deeply divided people.

What followed was in many senses an odd war, the kind we will probably not see again. Argentina and Britain had a long history of collaboration, and to many on both sides of the Atlantic it all came as a big surprise. This effect reached also a large number of the military that were to fight, but a mixture of professional ethos and the swiftness of events minimised the effects of the amazement.

On 2 April 1982, at around 22:30, Naval Special Forces landed in Soledad (East Falkland). I was then a lieutenant in the Agrupación de Buzos Tácticos (combat divers), and as such part of this group. Some eight hours later, badly wounded by British bullets, I lay at the side of my dying platoon leader and my participation in the war was over.

To many others, destiny was not so merciful. I can barely imagine the horror and anguish of a bombardment; the despair of the trenches; the filth; the cold and the misery. Nor can I grasp the gruesome agony of those unlucky ones whose ships and aeroplanes were sunk or destroyed. More than a thousand British and Argentine service personnel and civilians lost their lives during the war and an even larger number have since committed suicide or met an untimely ruin.

Wars are ugly affairs in which people break important patterns of behaviour, and this one also saw a few former enemies joining efforts behind the same cause. It could be said that despite all its misery it briefly offered a grim but effective way to heal a distressed society. Sadly enough, at the time this book was first published, few of my compatriots seemed to have taken the hint.

In a more general view, sometimes it seems to me that the war happened in another world, under a different code than the one we now live by. This was a war between two countries which share comparable cultural values and love freedom. In spite of a few crude and relatively ineffective propaganda stunts, the contenders were not dehumanised in the minds of their opponents and I still believe that hatred was never a major factor. It was not bitterness that drove either side against the other, as much as plain realism. It was a soldier's war with no civilian targets. Combat was close, it had a human scale.

This book was originally written in Spanish and with the Argentine public in mind. In that sense, I believe it calls for a little introduction in the English-speaking world and therefore, for those readers who may appreciate it, I offer below a very succinct account of Argentina's history until the war and its relation to the islands.

In 1816 Argentina declared its independence from Spain, and in 1823 the new republic took possession of the Malvinas islands, which had until then belonged to the Spanish crown, sending a governor and ninety settlers there in 1826. In 1833 Britain invaded the islands, ousted the Argentine governor, and set up a colony in Port Stanley.

Argentina's first Constitution was penned in 1853. A prolonged civil war held the country in unrest until the battle of Pavón in 1861 put an end to the fight.

Thereupon the country enjoyed sustained growth and relative political stability under a series of democratic governments until the 1929 Wall Street collapse destroyed the international status quo, fatally wounding the country's economy, which depended heavily on foreign trade.

In September 1930 a military coup removed the elected president, Hipólito Irigoyen. It was the first intromission of the military in government since Pavón, and from then on their participation became increasingly prominent as a series of *de facto* regimes (punctuated by attempts to return to democracy) continued, until 1946. In that year Colonel Perón, with the orchestrated support of unions and mobs, was elected president. A right-wing demagogue admirer of Franco and Mussolini, he was to hold office uninterrupted for almost ten years, characterised by increasing corruption, manipulative rhetoric and state supported jingoism. Though Argentina's claim about its sovereign rights upon the Malvinas had regularly and tenaciously been upheld in international fora, it was Perón who made the issue sink into the minds of the people and established it as a national cause.

Perón was deposed in 1955 through another military coup. The leaders of the revolution held power for three years before delivering it once again to a democratic government. Ten years (three presidencies) went by until the military came back to power in the figure of General Juan Carlos Onganía. This was 1966, the Cold War was at its height, and anti-communism was the call of the day. Many important democratic freedoms were limited, when not denied. Two other military dictators followed Onganía's repressive regime until the military grasp came to a brief pause in 1973 with the return of Perón from his Spanish exile.

Perón was now old, sick and ineffectual. If anything, his return served only to aggravate the confrontations that the last twenty years of repression had tried to silence through totalitarian measures. By 1974 Perón had died, leaving his third wife, María Estela "Isabel" Martínez, in charge. Inflation was mounting, the economy was in chaos, and riots were exploding everywhere. To make things worse, leftist guerilla groups which Perón had initially helped grow with a view to using them as supporters were spreading chaos throughout the land, growing stronger by the day and threatening to 'liberate' areas as large as provinces, sequestering them from control of the central government.

These groups had been developing since the early 1960s. They answered to a mix of ideologies and received significant support from abroad, with Cuba, China and the USSR as their most active supporters. Before jumping into the second phase of their mission – spearheaded by Che Guevara's failed attempt at establishing a victorious rural guerrilla war in Bolivia – they were active in major cities, operating through a network of cells whose members scarcely knew each other. While every now and then they staged carefully planned propaganda gatherings, secrecy and deception were prominent among their policies. Several of these organisations included cadres that had received training abroad (mainly in Cuba, Palestine, Libya and Angola) and their intelligence ability and combat capacity posed a very real threat to government forces. They kept substantial cash-flow through threats, extortion and kidnapping of wealthy or otherwise prominent persons; were technically speaking well equipped; and their efforts were mainly directed to weakening the police, the military and every other law enforcement organisation in order to reduce the state's influence and spread chaos, instill fear in the people, and gain power for the Cause. Most prominent among these groups were FAR (Revolutionary Armed Forces), ERP (People's Revolutionary Army) and Montoneros. In 1973, FAR and Montoneros became one organisation under the latter's name.

For most Argentines it was a dangerous and confusing time to live in. Carrying a gun was not unusual, tension was constant and everywhere was the danger of a bomb exploding potentially near you or being caught in the middle of a firefight. People lived in fear and it was never clear where threats would come from or whom one could trust. While the use of fake IDs was rampant – if not mandatory – among the guerrillas, most members of the military, the police and other law enforcement agencies were seldom seen in uniform. Equally, wearing uniform in public places was discouraged for cadets in military academies.

In October 1975, following a particularly vicious attack of Montoneros on the 29th Mountain Infantry Regiment in Formosa, the government of Isabel Perón issued three decrees ordering the Armed Forces 'to carry out all the military and security operations necessary to annihilate the action of subversive elements in all the territory of the Nation'. Congress immediately ratified the decrees, none of which was made public until 24 September 1983.

At the beginning of 1976 the country was riddled with

600% annual-rate inflation, riots and crimes were escalating, and terrorist activities were out of control. The administration was paralysed. On 26 March, answering demands from almost every political leader in the opposition and with strong public support, a military Junta took power, beginning the six-year long period named 'Process of National Reorganisation'.

It proved to be disastrous. To begin with, the Junta was made up of the three most senior officers of each force, the Army, the Navy and the Air Force. These three branches had a history of mutual mistrust and differed fundamentally in their philosophy and background.

While the Navy was – and still is – shaped around Nelsonian values, the Army was modeled on the pattern of the German soldier. While the Navy was traditionally and fiercely anti-Perónist, the Army was split. The Air Force was mistrusted by both the Navy and the Army. A 'newcomer' created under Perón, its members were often referred to as 'pancakes' by the other two branches, in reference to their ability to 'turn upside-down' in the air. The infamous moniker dates back to 16 June 1955, when a group of military and civilians opposing Perón's regime – which was far from democratic – tried to stage a coup and kill the president. During the attack, naval planes bombed and strafed the iconic Plaza de Mayo, facing the Government Palace, killing 380 and wounding around 700. The Air Force planes accompanying them were supposed to do their share, but in a tardy show of loyalty to Perón, they decided not to use their weapons and just flew over the plaza. To their credit, they were to prove their valour beyond everyone's expectations during the Malvinas war.

This lack of trust between services reached to all

ranks and was not a good start. Additionally, personalities played a crucial role in the Junta. General Videla, chief of the Army, was a dedicated professional of strong Catholic conviction. He was an honest soldier, and lacked the political abilities the task claimed. Admiral Massera, chief of the Navy, was another animal altogether: smart, charismatic and with an agenda of his own, he was ruthless and ambitious. Unlike Videla, he was popular both with the officers and the ranks, and had craftily and patiently raised the loyalty of a group of senior officers whom had turned almost to uncond-itional. He disliked Videla's cautious ways but was very much aware of the Army's importance as the largest armed force. Historic revisionism has revealed that, aside from several well-known efforts to get Perón's blessings while being already chief of the Navy, he also carried out negotiations with the top cats of several terrorist organisations.

To fight the urban guerrillas who were growing stronger by the day, the Junta resorted to unconventional fighting methods that had been learned at officer-level courses in French-occupied Algiers and in CIA training camps in Central America, and had been practised in the 1950s in conflicts that were by then almost forgotten. These were, after all, the seventies.

What started as a dim light at the end of the tunnel of Argentine politics soon turned into a very dark night. While still adhering in principle to the initial aim of returning government to the people as soon as possible, successive Juntas proved their lack of competence to administer the State, while the already fragmented base of the deposed political structure continued to weaken under every possible kind of repressive measure.

By 1981, General Leopoldo Fortunato Galtieri led the Junta as chief of the Army. His Junta co-member, Admiral Isaac Anaya, had been long obsessed with the idea of returning the Malvinas to national sovereignty. Driven by a combination of Anaya's enthusiasm and demands, growing social unrest and the apparent inability of the British government to answer the country's claims for sovereignty over the Malvinas, he ordered the creation of a plan to retake the islands. It was initially to be carried out in late 1982, but complications (widely published since) made Operation Rosario take place earlier.

What followed was the war, brief and brutal. In the end Argentina capitulated, but still holds to the claim that the Malvinas islands are Argentine. In the meantime the population of the islands – in some cases over six generations old – has entered the game with a strong and growing voice. Though in the fluid arena of international politics it seems futile to try to foresee what the future may bring, it will certainly be constructed with regards to the memory of the many valiant men who fell in those cold months of 1982.

All characters in the stories that follow are fictional, though they reflect thoughts and behaviours that I believe would have been typical of the persons described.

Finally, I hope this book offers an insight into a special period of Argentine history. I think it describes a way of thinking that – for good or bad – is no more. Our world pushes forward and technology, ideology, economy and political convenience have transformed a great deal of the ethical landscape in which I grew up. Sometimes it seems to me that once the Berlin wall finally came down we were meant to accept that almost anything is explicable and – in the larger view – acceptable. We have lived, and we live longer. We should make it worthwhile.

Diego García Quiroga
Oslo, 1 February 2016

Javier

'Alright! I don't know how he did it!' said Tomás, and I could swear he lifted his arm as he tried to fend off our objections.

'But he sure wasn't cheating,' he insisted, already a little fed up. 'Elena was there too, and we were pretty close to the guy. Besides, once he was done we went backstage and tried to find if there was anything phony there, but we found nothing…'

No one answered him, we had already lost interest and in any case we knew he was telling the story just for the sake of talking and to avoid thinking, because even though we were all scared shitless, the worst thing was to realize how fucking lonely you were. We had already grown used to the cold and the dampness and we had stopped caring for the muck and the dirt and the walls that stank like rotten dung.

The Brits bombed our position once again and everyone reacted as usual. As soon as the explosions began we would crouch hugging our stomachs, squeezing closer to the next guy in order to deal better with the blasts that seemed to dislodge your bones. Talking would become impossible. Actually it was possible, but you couldn't hear shit. We closed our eyes and tried to fix our thoughts on something, but it felt as if your skull was being hammered from all directions. We couldn't do anything. It was as cold as hell and we were trapped, each of us with his own terror. In the end you would just fall asleep.

During the breaks we would scream to each other and

talk about anything, as if to confirm that we were still alive. It would not start right away. But when the bombing was over we would still hear the sound of explosions for a while and, although we knew they were not for real, we sat just listening to the memory of the blasts. Afterwards you heard a buzz, as if someone kept whistling in your ear.

Presently Gatica started laughing. It wasn't easy to see and too dark to make out faces, but I could tell it was him because of his special laugh. He was dark and slim and his eyes sat too close together like on a mouse. I'm sure all of us knew that he laughed because Tomás had mentioned his sister again. But at this stage we had already bonked in our minds all the girls the platoon knew, so nobody paid attention – not even Tomás.

I didn't know him very well, but always thought I would have liked to meet him somewhere else. He seemed to be an okay guy. He lived in Caballito, close to the statue of El Cid. Before the war I used to date a girl from the same neighbourhood and went out with her a couple of times. I never mentioned it to him. You never know, do you?

She was a skinny blonde and she was game and great in making out. But it was hard to notice at first sight with that angel face of hers. I've heard it say that Buenos Aires was quite a screwed-up place then, and I remember the old folk were constantly at us, insisting that we ought to be careful. The fact is that we never saw the danger, as we were busy jumping from bed to bed and not really ruled by schedules. Every now and then you would hear about some really fucked-up thing that you had missed by sheer luck, and then you thought that life was just like that: a crappy deal for those who got fucked. One just didn't go out looking for unnecessary complications.

Patricia. That was her name. Patricia. She had a sister who was a real pain. I think a cop had raped her or something like that...

Our Sergeant's name was Coronel and he had a bunch of stories from those years. We had no way of knowing whether they were real but, as the guy didn't appear to have much in terms of imagination, they could well have been true. Every time he talked about those days he would refer to them as 'the tough times' and suddenly become silent as if it pained him to remember. But I think it was all just to show off.

Or 'the iron years', he also loved that one. The military are fascinated by these terms and when they use them they believe they are back there in 'Nam, or that they can be pals with Schwarzenegger. Coronel was this type of bloke and at the beginning we laughed behind his back, also because being a Sergeant and having Coronel for a surname is sort of silly. But he was not as dangerous as he could have been. Before we arrived in the hole we heard about how things were in other sections, in other platoons and under other Sergeants. It was full of motherfuckers out there. Coronel was fairly decent. He was a nobody, but a decent one.

It was late in the day, and the light was fading fast. As I said, it was already impossible to make out the faces, but you get used to it. You get used to the cold, to the smell, to the slimy floor and the snores of those who fall asleep, tired of shaking. Then they look as good as dead. And you have to sit quite still, you cannot see shit and each one sketches out a mental map of his position. At that stage we had no torches. We had drained all the fucking batteries days before, and all you saw around you were shadows.

The place was so full that if you moved you could end

up shoving your boot into another guy's face and then it would be chaos, for it is similar with dominoes – when you move a piece you shove the next one that bumps against another, and that one bumps another and so it goes on until the last one is shoved without even having seen it coming. Once it happened exactly like that, and Coronel threatened everybody by throwing us out of the hole and letting us freeze to death.

Now that I think about it, I wonder why any of us didn't come up with the idea of putting a bullet through the guy's neck and have him stop all his nagging and shouting. He probably never thought about it himself, but it could have happened.

Until we arrived in the hole I used to have a different idea of the war. As soon as we landed on the Islands we knew there was an enemy to fight against, and that created a special tension. We were here to fuck them good. And let them fear us also, because we were keen.

After a while, though, it all went to hell. Once in the hole we knew that we were going nowhere and were just waiting for something big to happen. Perhaps they would just come and shoot us. Or perhaps a Brit would suddenly appear in the entrance of the hole and shout something like, 'You can go home, the exercise is over!' To most of us it felt as if time itself had stopped. We didn't have a clue what was going on outside.

In the beginning we had a Lieutenant and that served as a distraction for us. He was a young fellow with red hair, and good-looking really. His name was Rafael Paunero and he was seriously Catholic. He went everywhere with a rosary in his hand and used to call us his *soldiers of Christ* and other bullshit like that. One afternoon he stepped on a buried mine and afterwards we couldn't even find his boots. Coronel was left to lead us, and I have no doubt that it was to his great surprise because he barely knew where we were, and certainly knew fuck all about where we should have been. But what was clear was that we were starving.

Coronel was starving too, and in order to make time go by faster we would talk about foods we liked and tried to remember how they tasted. But it was not easy. I couldn't remember the taste of walnuts, for example. We were busy with this when we discovered the hole.

That night Tomás began telling this story about the performer they had seen at the circus. Almost all of his stories included other members of his family, and this one was no exception. He had this sister that he always went on about until we gave him so much shit that we made him stop. The story he was telling this time had happened somewhere in Santa Fé, where they had both been spending some days at one of his aunts. One afternoon they learned that an amusement park was visiting town and there would be kiosks with games, shooting ranges, a merry-go-round, a small ferris wheel and even a circus arena under a tent.

He said that the fair meant a lot for the town, which made me think the place must have been really tiny. Then he felt the need to inform us that his sister was not exactly fond of circuses, and launched into a long explanation of how clowns made her especially sad on account of a film she had seen when she was small and that had made her cry.

But the core story was that they had seen this contortionist, a chap who, according to Tomás, was capable of bending to extremes and who could also swallow impossible things such as a wristwatch, key ring and pair of glasses. When he mentioned the glasses there was a reaction, possibly because we had already had enough.

'Bullshit!' cried someone, and immediately we were all certain that nobody can swallow a pair of glasses. Tomás swore it was totally possible. He had himself witnessed it. It had been one of those slim pairs of reading glasses.

'Not a pair of Ray Bans, you asshole!' he said to nobody in particular, trying to defend his story.

In the end some voices said it was okay and were even ready to let him carry on, but opinions were still heavily split. He knew we weren't happy with the story, and so told how the guy had carefully folded the glasses, securing them with scotch tape. He also tried to explain the way he had stretched his neck upwards to ease the swallowing. This elevated the story's veracity a bit, although he was obviously running out of arguments when Gatica, who was still laughing, got a bit braver and asked:

'And your sister... does she also swallow glasses, your sister?'

Gatica was some bad motherfucker. I had seen him doing the same thing to Tomás a couple of times already. He bit and held fast as a bulldog. Anyway I think that Tomás may have hit him with the butt of his rifle, because Gatica let out a cry and, simultaneously, Tomás' gun fired.

A gun fired inside an enclosed space makes an awesome noise and leaves your ears buzzing like forever. It stank of cordite and loose earth and everybody was shouting, so it was impossible to know what was going on until we first heard Coronel's voice over the din.

He was in a rage, shouting, 'Fucking arse-holes! The one thing we need now is for one of you retards to kill one of us or have us all killed by giving away our position, you motherfuckers! What the fuck d'you think you're doing?' and other niceties of the same type. I could also hear Ramirez's high-pitched, hysterical laugh. Ramirez found everything funny, as little girls do.

At last Coronel piped down and, on his order, we carried out a head count, each one calling his name aloud. The first to speak was Fabbriani, sitting by the entrance. We were all alive.

Then Coronel called: 'Salinas! Stick your head out and see whether you can detect any activity out there! For all we know, this asshole here may have woken up the whole Island!'

I heard the *ras-ras-ras* of Salinas as he crawled his way to the entrance, and thought that this time the Sergeant had pulled a cheap one. Putting your head out was always dangerous and he could well have picked on Fabbriani, who was already there.

But everybody was on Salinas, also Coronel.

He came from La Plata, Salinas, and looked like a dork. He had a face like a cow. He was not much of a talker and his dad was a history teacher. I guess there he had gathered some incredible information about the Islands, as if he had studied them for an exam. It was as if he had been told in advance that we were all going to be sent to fight this shitty war and had written a paper on every fucking place that we landed on.

He could have been better advised, though, for his knowledge was not universally appreciated. Once he launched into a speech about Gaucho Rivero, the bloke they say once stood up for Argentine rights over the Islands.

'Rivero,' Salinas explained, 'was one of the ranch workers who stayed on the Islands when the British displaced Vernet. Vernet had been the Governor, appointed by Buenos Aires.'

So far there was nothing wrong in what he said and some of the guys were surprised to learn how ancient the affair was, for in the barracks back home we had had such a load of Gaucho Rivero that many thought that this story had happened just yesterday.

Salinas was well informed and he knew how to tell a story. But all peace came to an end when he went on to explain the murders of the loser that replaced Vernet and those who sided with him, all of whom were dispatched by Rivero in a murky incident.

The Lieutenant was still among us and Salinas had the bad luck to have him listen, for Paunero was a member of the *Compañía de Comandos,*[*] a group notorious for their Christian chauvinism. So the very moment he heard Salinas telling us that Gaucho Rivero was a criminal, Paunero's face turned as red as a beetroot and he let out a bellow that stunned us all and made us brace for what would follow. Poor Salinas went silent immediately and turned as white as paper as the Lieutenant got closer, until their noses were almost touching, rather in the manner you see Drill Sergeants do in US Marines' movies. Then he exploded:

'I will teach you respect for our heroes, you useless piece of shit, you faggot!' he shouted in the poor chap's face. 'We are here only because of people like Rivero, who wouldn't let the English pirates trample the sovereign rights of our Motherland!'

After the Lieutenant left, a bunch of us agreed that this argument was bullshit and weird. No one except that crazy son of a bitch could have really wanted to be there. Anyway, once he had finished thrashing poor Salinas, he

* 601 Commando Company, Argentine Army.

turned to face us. We were all very quiet and I guess we were looking at him as if mesmerised, in awe that this type of cretin could be for real.

'And all of you,' he shouted, 'get it in your heads that ours is a sacred mission! The crap this little shit repeats was written by British motherfuckers. They have always tried to discredit the Motherland and rob what is ours!'

He was completely beside himself and, before leaving, issued an order that I thought deserved to be framed because it was so preposterous: he forbade us from letting ourselves be convinced by Salinas' sissy-talk!

Fortunately these attacks of flag-waving verbosity were short. Maybe it was because our faces told him that we totally bought it, as they consisted almost exactly of the same crap we had been told when still on the mainland. When they happened, and once he got tired of screaming, he would take off as if escaping from lepers and then, from a distance, would bark orders to Coronel.

But the Salinas-Rivero issue didn't end there: from then on, and every time he caught sight of the guy from La Plata, Lieutenant Paunero would explode into a new sermon against traitors and turncoats, among whom I bet he had started to include historians.

The thing is that that evening Salinas poked his head back into the hole and said:

'Sergeant, I can't see shit.'

Coronel corrected him.

'Speak properly, private!' he said, and you could tell the edginess in his voice. 'I know you can't see shit. Do you think I'm an idiot? It's night-time, what the fuck did you expect to see? 9 de Julio Avenue, perhaps?'

He went on like that for a while, chuckling like an idiot, preying on Salinas and upsetting everybody, for it was plain to see that the bang from Tomás' gun had worried him quite a bit. Precisely him, on whom for good or bad our fate depended.

I believe I'm not mistaken if I tell you that we believed Coronel had some military capability. Nevertheless none of us reflected on the fact that his experience was restricted to depots and barracks.

He was a chairborne Ranger, a military clerk. It's like any paper-pusher in a public office, with the difference that you wear uniform and a rank insignia. This is not necessarily for the better. Anybody knows that most of those who work in a public office fuck up the service deliberately and screw their clients because they don't dare play *macho* inside. Dress these people in patterned cammies and you've just got the right picture.

Coronel had an advantage in that he came from Chaco. That made him on the one hand not so evil and, on the other, a silent sufferer. But in spite of this he wasn't an easy-going chap. True, he overdid it with his silences and we lived under the impression that he actually hated us. There was something cunning – almost servile – when he kept staring after issuing an order, as if waiting for you to dodge it and give him a chance to release his frustration.

That night he was scared. At least that was our impression. You could say that that put him closer to us, for we were permanently in panic. To make things worse, Corporal D'Amico was outside on one of his scouting tours. We all suspected that each time D'Amico said he'd go scouting it was only because he wanted to get some fresh air. In any case, he was a strange chap. He talked little and didn't pay us any attention, even though he was supposed to work as a link between the Sergeant and us.

Anyway, all the shit the Sergeant directed to Salinas

that night signalled the end of any harmony we could have expected after the bombing.

It feels weird when the guy who gives the orders is afraid. Even though normally I didn't pay more attention to Coronel's attitude than to anybody else's, he was, after all, responsible for the platoon and nobody could think of orders coming from elsewhere. But orders for what? That was the thing! We'd been in that hole for days already and didn't have a fucking clue about anything. There was no way for us to know whether we were inside enemy territory or safe behind our lines. Once the Lieutenant vaporised, the clerk Coronel had been left without a compass, so to speak.

Once we located the hole – or once we stumbled into it, for that's actually what happened – we had a couple of days with their nights when the bombing was almost continuous. Hungry as we were, soiling our pants because of the cold and dying of sleep, no one cared too much whether whatever was happening outside was the prelude to a British attack or the silence of death. It did not matter.

I have since realised that it was not the Brits who were killing us, but our own imbecility. It was our disorganisation, our lack of preparation to endure those shitty conditions. It felt hopeless. Everything was a mess!

We were stuck inside a stinking hole and none of us could even remember the last time he had eaten a warm meal. We bumped against each other like rats slithering on the slime on which we laid, drenched in sweat that eventually froze to flux once again into the fabric of our uniforms. They soon turned into rags that weren't even good enough to make us warm.

When Salinas brushed my legs as he felt his way in

the darkness I had the impulse to grip his arm and tell him that everything was all right, that it was not his fault that we were stuck inside that reeking hell, that the Sergeant was a sorry dick shitting his pants out of fear, a simple Joe who otherwise didn't have a clue about anything. But Coronel did not give me the chance.

'Let's go outside,' he said.

If it hadn't been for the darkness that prevented us from even spotting a girl's ass, as Ahumada used to say between amazing hoots that made him sound like a badly-drunk hooker, I would swear we all looked pretty baffled, unable to believe our ears. Holy shit, the man had initiative! It was indeed some news!

First man out was Virasoro, always silent and with his face remorseful as if he had just wet himself. Behind him followed Coronel and then the rest, everybody anxious to get out in the night's air. The bomb or whatever it was exploded just as the last guy – Vergara – was exiting.

I remember only the blast, a blinding white light and total silence. I didn't feel panic. I was just sure that I was dead because nothing came out from my mouth when I tried to speak. I saw Coronel's arm fall in a neat parabola and bounce on the ground very close to me. I saw it all perfectly. I recognised the watch still on the wrist, its bright green face that had always reminded me of the wings of a beetle. I saw it go by with impossible slowness and tumble silently among the rocks.

Somehow shocked, I thought that the platoon was probably dead to a man. It was then that I felt a dull pain in my knee, a sort of bony discomfort. I can't tell how I realised that I was falling, and I tried to grab someone or something that was at my side.

Then everything disappeared.

The River

'... In any case, it was highly improbable that anyone could spot it from that distance. The whole Brigade was standing on parade and it was so hot that surely even the big shots under the canopy had their brains as fried as ours, not to mention those who didn't have a cover.

'I pulled the rifle up as carefully as I could until I had it resting on the webbing belt and... I can't tell you what a relief it was to feel the blood flowing once again! Sometimes your arm would still be hurting the day after.

'No,' he reflected shaking his head to back his words, 'it wasn't easy to keep the Mauser at shoulder position.

'The Naval Area Commander was visiting the Academy that day. He was one of these guys who love to hear their own voice. He would talk and talk as if there was no tomorrow, like those commercial aircraft pilots who cut the transmission right in the middle of the movie to inform you of bullshit no one really cares about or everybody already knows, like the aircraft's ETA. Probably they feel entitled to those ten minutes of fame, and so they wax on about anything in order not to miss the chance.

'Since very early that day, the concrete of the courtyard was as hot as boiler pipes and I kept twitching my toes inside my shoes to prevent them from burning. But the parade was proving to be extremely long. After the speeches came the awards presentation, once again with our rifles at shoulder arms. At this stage almost every single guy in the formation was counting each step taken by those approaching to receive their award. It was a lousy forty metres, but it seemed to take them ages. Then it was a Chinese torture to watch them salute, grab the medal and diploma, shake hands, salute once again, make a perfect about-turn and slowly return to their place. It was like watching a movie in slow motion.

'Back then I used to hate parades, but when I entered the Academy I was all for them. I could even say that I was seized by patriotic enthusiasm when I saw the impeccably-aligned rows go by and the gloved hands moving up and down to the rhythm of the band.

'For me, marching was the best part of the show. It started when the band took its place at the centre. Then came the Brigade march-on. It really was a sight, believe me, the uniforms profiled against the Academy's park that looked like a golf course, the swords and the buckles gleaming and all that martial music in your ears.

'Anyway, that afternoon I was fed up as the Admiral kept on talking, interrupting the award presentation with more and more comments. At last I heard "Order, arms!" and, as I tried to lower the rifle, it fell forward when my arm gave way. I reacted in panic, even today I cannot explain how I managed to stop it before it hit the ground. I finished the movement almost on time with the rest of the line and thought I had cleared it, but then I heard a voice behind me: "Get out of the line and follow me!"

'I took a step backwards. Fraga, who was right behind me, stepped over to cover me and I followed the *Russian*. We walked past the end of the formation and continued towards the river beyond the trees, oblivious of the parade. At the waterside he ordered me to hit the ground and start doing push-ups. The order was outrageous and I didn't obey it right away. You see, the son of a bitch was perfectly aware that I would mess up my uniform and I needed it in order to go on leave the day after.

He insisted, it was plain that he wasn't joking. I let the rifle rest against a tree and got on my knees, but the concrete was blazing hot and I straightened up to try the turf instead, but the psycho pointed to the concrete and said:

'Over here, sissy! Get on with it!'

'I touched the concrete and I swear to you that I'll never forget it. It was like touching a red-hot plate. I pulled my hands back instantly, but the skin was already charred. Knowing that nobody could spot us behind the cover of the trees, the son of a bitch looked at me and repeated the order. He hissed it. He didn't even blink.

'Begin, you wimp!' he said.

'I wanted to believe he was joking. He really couldn't be such an asshole to allow me to burn my hands to the bone! But there was I with my belly on the ground, arms held up and charred hands in the air. I could feel my chest was beginning to feel the heat and, before I could react, *Russian* stepped on my hands, pressing them against the concrete, as he shouted at me to begin.

'I yelled like a hog on the hook. I forgot the parade, the band, my uniform, everything. I could feel the blisters grow on my palms, only to burst and develop anew. I pulled desperately and got one of my hands free and, just as I pounded like a madman the leg that still held the other fast, one of *Russian*'s classmates showed up. He had heard my scream.

'"What's going on up here?" he asked as I retrieved my hand when the pressure weakened. He was senior to *Russian*.

'"Nothing," answered the bastard with a shrug, "this cadet's a little soft. He thinks he's cool enough to cheat at shoulder arms and pull it off and, when I order him to give me some push-ups, he is concerned about getting his palms scorched."

'The guy looked at my palms and ordered me to go to sick-bay and report to him later. As I was leaving he advised me to avoid being stopped by an officer, and then turned to address my tormenter.

'That's the way things were then,' concluded Eduardo.

Sitting on the stones of the wharf, their legs swinging lazily above the water, the ex-naval officer and *Numa* did their best not to mind the swarms of afternoon mosquitoes.

'It was as simple as that,' continued Eduardo. 'There was no room for complaints. His little prank cost me twenty-three days of going around with my hands bandaged like a fucking scarecrow. I had to have them dressed twice a day and there were times I would have liked to kill the guy, but you weren't there to take revenge on anybody. If it hurt, you just swallowed it. Nobody was forced to sign on. It was a voluntary choice. And I could say that I chose to stay mainly to prove that I was hard enough. Maybe that was the whole point, for each time you felt like calling it a day there would be a senior cadet around reminding you that a ferry sailed from the Island every twenty minutes. The fact is that you needed to be sort of nuts to be there.

'With time, you learned that everybody had been through more or less the same shit. Everyone carried his share of hatred that gradually shrunk to nothing, for you end up accepting that four years of chicken-coop law may make some sense after all. I think they bond you to the others, test your limits and offer some evidence of your endurance, of how long you are willing to be stretched. The level of attrition was interesting. In the course of those four years many would give up and leave, fed up with the idea of screwing their thumbs for values that either they didn't share or wouldn't accept.

'For it's all a matter of faith, you see? You have to believe that all that crap has a purpose. If you can't do that, you'd better leave.'

He took a sip from the beer in his hand.

'And you believed it,' said *Numa*, asserting rather than asking.

'Of course I did! How else could I have loved it? But I can't be so wrong, for there's still bunches of people out there willing to join the military.'

'And what d'you think those guys are after?' asked *Numa*.

'I don't know,' answered Eduardo, 'but I believe there is a mystique there, a sense of belonging that you don't find elsewhere. Don't forget that being in the military gives you the chance of doing things very few people can do otherwise. Things that are sometimes scary and that many may wish not to have to deal with, but which in the end someone has to do. It's a team adventure. That is why I don't call it a career. You're not in there to win over anybody.'

Eduardo spoke with conviction, and he loved an audience.

'Maybe I'm just like that,' thought *Numa*, reflecting on his friend's words. 'Maybe it's a perspective that is not easy to forget.'

'Would you go back in?' he asked.

Eduardo didn't answer right away. He stood up and threw the empty bottle into a nearby rubbish bin.

'You can't go back, *Numa*. I've changed, and the Navy that once was is not there any more.' He raised the collar of his jacket and started to walk towards the town centre.

It had begun to blow. *Numa* lit a cigarette before following behind.

It was getting dark. They had spent all day wandering the cobble-stoned streets that run close to the waterfront, and now they ambled through the beach towards the clubhouse. Eduardo recounted his first year as an officer.

'I arrived at noon sharp and the ship wasn't there,' he said, waving his arm to underline how alarmed he had been not to find his unit moored.

'My first ship, and I was coming late! Nobody had told me that the second phase of the Antarctic Campaign had been shortened because of the rotten weather in the Drake. As a result, the blokes in the Hydrographic Office had arranged for a supplementary voyage to be taken as soon as the conditions allowed it. Typically, somebody forgot telling the Naval detailer about this and I ended up showing up exactly one day after the ship had sailed. I had spent the morning taking my physical at the Naval hospital and, on arrival, I only found a sentry booth with a handwritten sign hanging inside showing the liberty dateline for the night before.

'Luckily there was another Naval ship on the same quay, one of these river-patrol crafts. As I considered my next step, an officer appeared on deck. Seeing me, he asked 'Mendoza?' and disappeared through a hatch before I was able to answer. He was back in no time with a brown envelope and gave it to me. 'Your orders!'

'I hadn't said a word, and for a moment I toyed with the idea of opening the orders there and then, read them and saying something like "I'm very sorry, this is really interesting but my name is Suárez", but he was a First Lieutenant and probably wouldn't find it very amusing. Just then a cab arrived and out of it came three girls.

They were pretty and kept chatting and laughing non-stop.

'"Guests," said the Lieutenant, "mind if I leave you now?"

'And he left me there standing on the pier. Once again I considered pretending to be another. Mendoza could have shown up anytime that morning, taken a look at the sign in the sentry booth, made up his mind and left. It wouldn't have sounded too odd to a Naval officer, but it was clear that the Lieutenant would be the sacrificial goat and, with things as they were, it wasn't unthinkable that my little joke would end up being treated as a serious security breach. New procedures were just being set up throughout the Navy and I would soon learn the importance of security. I didn't know the guy and there was a big chance he would be blamed. In the end I decided to play it straight.

'The orders were addressed to *Mr Midshipman Dn. Eduardo Mendoza* and I remember that this minimal hint of acknowledgement made me feel proud. There I was, not yet twenty-four, and already being addressed with a certain gravity. Today it seems nothing special, but back then it felt good, as if I had achieved something that others also desired. The envelope was stamped *CONFIDENTIAL* and, although that was the norm with all communications related to personnel, it also felt weird to see my whereabouts treated as confidential. Even though that had nothing to do with me, it was anyway quite cool.

'After mentioning that the ship had had to sail at an earlier date, there followed orders for me to show up at a police station at Tigre in the shortest possible time. I was to make contact with constable Sansimón and he would explain everything. I had to show up in civilian clothes and refrain from telling anybody that I would be working there. The entire thing suggested adventure, so without thinking twice I walked up to Retiro and took the coastal train.

'I didn't have a clue about what to expect but I imagined my job would have something to do with counter-terrorism. Aside from some lectures we received in the Academy and what was said in the papers or the TV, I knew little about that war. We had an idea of what went on in the street but we didn't know how big it was, even though we saw that things were far from normal. This also influenced our lives.

'For example, the details of every trip we took had to be kept secret. It was common to see liberty delayed because of bomb alerts to the ferries that linked the Academy to the mainland. Then there were inspections of the buses and trains we used, and we often lost a lot of time. It was also forbidden to go to some places in uniform.

'Of course, all this added to the natural lack of confidence between the civilians and us. When and why it started I don't know, but back then we got bad looks almost anywhere we went. We didn't trust civilians and they didn't trust us.'

'Yes,' said *Numa*. 'I sort of remember that.' He had been silent most of the afternoon. He wanted to listen to what his friend had to stay. They had not seen each other for quite some time and he was curious about the way life had worked on Eduardo's points of view. He remembered him as someone always in line with his convictions, but he also knew people can change.

'I remember it well,' he added. 'It had always been there. Nobody ever thought much of the military. But it ended in open hatred.'

'My point exactly!' agreed Eduardo. 'We were the scumbags. In the Academy one could see that something was fucked up, but I had never really seen the problem clearly. We heard of things that happened to guys we knew: so-and-so had been gunned down, another guy was in reality a double agent, someone else's wife was friends with the terrorists, and other stories like that. Some of them were true. You could tell those that had been made up to build morale.

'And most of us were mainly concerned with our lives on the island, which – as I told you – was quite an environment. But I'm losing the thread… in Tigre I took a walk enjoying the sun. It was early and I was not in a hurry. I was hungry and soon found a place to eat, for I didn't know what would happen once I got to the police station.

'I sat by the window. I was getting in the mood and saw a potential criminal in every face. There weren't a lot of people, but soon five men arrived wearing these overalls that public workers use when they work in the street.

'They were really big and one of them looked vaguely familiar. I was sure he knew me too, for he winked at me and raised a finger to his mouth as to signal silence. They picked a table and he sat with his back towards me. Then the moment I heard him speak I lost all doubt. He was Lovak. He was the *Russian*.

'I had not seen the cunt since he had graduated and had almost forgotten him. I felt the old anger rising, but I could understand that there was something more important going on than a foolish cadet story, and played dumb as I listened from behind my menu card.'

'And what are you going to order here?' asked *Numa*, taking a seat. 'I remember you were fond of scrambled eggs and here they serve them as we like them. We might be across the river now, but Uruguayans are more *criollos* than Gardel ever was.'

Eduardo looked at him over the rim of his bi-focals. 'It's been so damn fucking long, *Numa*!'

He was beaming.

'Let's order a couple of beers to begin with!'

Numa hailed the waiter, who pointed at the two beer bottles he was balancing on the tray. *Numa* nodded and Eduardo went back to his story.

'When I left the bar the *Russian* and his friends were still at it. I had heard him calling for ketchup a couple of times and was not surprised that that was all, for he was not much of a talker.

'I spent a while looking at the boats on the quay and eventually climbed into one that was just about to sail, though it looked as if only a miracle would keep it from sinking. I told the man my destination, paid my fare and sat on the life vests that doubled as seats.

'I still wondered what the *Russian* was doing over there. I had paid close attention to their talk during my lunch and was no wiser. Though in that costume it would have been impossible to tell he was a Naval officer, I had no doubts that it was him.

'But it took us almost an hour to reach the police station, and I stopped thinking about him as I tried to learn the landmarks of the many islands and channels.'

The waiter arrived with the beers and *Numa* proposed ordering something to eat.

'You gentlemen care to try the day's special?' asked the waiter.

'Yes,' said Eduardo. 'Make it the day's special. Surely it will last longer.'

'In any case we may order something else afterwards,

right?' asked *Numa*.

'Of course! We have all night!' answered Eduardo, topping up the glasses before resuming his story.

'The station was by the Capitán river. A flat building with badly washed walls. It's still there. There were no inner doors, so that you got the impression of being in a long hall. It was at the end of a little path, past a rusty flagpole stuck on a concrete block with a police shield on it. It was getting dark, the lights inside were on and there were a couple of sergeants and a man in civvies. They sat drinking *mate** around a desk.

'I entered and the civilian stood up and stretched out his hand, saying "Welcome to Fort Alamo!" It was Raúl Sansimón. He had smoked me out straight away, he said, because anybody could have told I was military from a mile's distance. He knew what the Navy was doing against terrorism. When I asked where he got his information he answered that that was precisely his job. He had been working undercover for seven years. We were on buddy terms from the start. He was about forty and was married to a judge's daughter.

'We worked together for almost eight weeks and I never learned so many things that I'd rather have not known. He taught me the street rules. It was then I learned to mistrust.'

The waiter came with the order and the friends kept talking as the restaurant filled up. The day's special was bigger than they had expected and they were happy to order just coffee afterwards. It was already night when they left and there were people hanging around the doors of bars, waiting for empty tables.

'As I said before,' resumed Eduardo, 'working with

* Infusion, and the small gourd it is served in.

the cops made me aware of things I didn't know even though they were all around me. I could say I learned to see. We worked long hours and ate when we were hungry. We patrolled circuits that were more or less fixed and normally made some extra rounds just to show the flag, hoping to discourage mischief.

'The people who lived on the Islands were used to our presence. If we were late they would come around to find out if something had happened. Most of them were old folks and their properties were no big thing, but there were also some very fine houses that were used only during the summer and went empty for the rest of the year. These were important buildings, with well-kept gardens and serious docks. We would check them at random, looking for any signs of theft or squatting, for it was very easy to break in through a window without anybody noticing.

'Once we came to a hotel run by a young German. I had seen him at the station and was aware that Raúl and the two sergeants, Corporal Brete and Corporal Agosti, called on him regularly. He had people come in during the weekend and Raúl offered him rides every time he needed something from the town. He said he did it to have a chance to talk to the guy, for the German loved to gossip and he would tell him everything he had seen. He had a woman, the German. I never met her. He also had a rowing boat.

'Once, ten or fifteen days after I arrived in the station, we saw a big motorboat moored to the pier of the hotel. It was late. The sun had already gone down. Nobody seemed to be on board and, as we got to her side, Raúl put on his gun belt. I asked him what was up and, instead of answering, he told me to stay in the boat with Brete and call HQ in the radio if I heard shots. As he and Agosti jumped on the pier, I made the boat fast.

'Behind me, Brete slipped over the side and into the water and started swimming slowly away, holding his head out. I didn't have a clue about what had alerted them, or what they wanted me to do.

'Then Raúl showed up at the door and motioned me to join him. As I got near he said that there seemed to be nobody on the island, but he was still speaking in whispers. Apparently somebody had raided the place and taken most of the things, even the cat's litter basket. He added that whoever it was had left in a bad mood, for the place was badly wrecked and they had vandalised all the furniture.

'Right then we heard a shot coming from behind the building, there where the German kept a chicken coop. It sounded like a .45 and I thought immediately of Brete. Agosti came running out from the house and we heard a second shot, this time followed by a shout and the sound of an outboard motor revving.

'It was pitch dark under the tree canopy, and we soon found Brete panting behind a fallen log. He had seen four persons and shot one as they climbed onto a boat. He thought he had killed the guy, for he had seen the body sink. He had recognised the German because of his gait but said the woman was not there, and someone had fired at him when he ordered the group to stop. Then he answered with his gun and saw a man fall in the water while the others escaped.

'He said they were big and seemed to be dressed in overalls like the ones public workers use when they work on the streets. He also said that he had seen an overall on the big motorboat. We returned to our boat and Raúl called HQ for a team of divers and ordered a search to locate the escape boat.

'Brete was right. There was an orange overall on the floor of the big boat. It was like those that *Russian* and his company had been wearing at the restaurant, and Brete had mentioned four big guys. You see I had a problem, for if *Russian* was working undercover for the Navy the coppers may not have had a clue, and it was not me who was going to blow it. On the other hand, if he was in league with criminals it meant I had always been right and he was just your usual piece of shit. But then, I had no way of knowing...

'So it was then,' he said as he distractedly opened a pack of cigarettes, 'that I discovered the real world and started looking at things differently, I guess. I later heard that it was the German's girl who delivered him to the Monta,* They had come to finish him that night but changed their mind. He was no big player and killing him would just bring them problems.

'One grew quite skeptical. I kept my mouth shut because I didn't trust my own buddies. I still don't know if it was the right thing to do. Perhaps I had this stupid idea that you couldn't trust a cop the way you did a Navy officer, or something like that.'

They walked to the hotel, talking about the things they did after leaving the Navy. It was long since each had gone their way: the war was now over and so was Eduardo's failed attempt to build a family. *Numa* had had his escapades to Brazil, then Venezuela and finally Puerto Madryn. They had kept irregular contact, happy just to know where the other one was. Every now and then they would touch base to check that they still understood each other and could reach across if needed. If the years weighed on them it didn't show and they had

* Montoneros.

still so many things to tell each other that they could have easily kept talking all night.

'Did you ever see *Russian* again?' asked Numa as they got the keys to their rooms.

'Yes, I saw him again a few times. But we never worked together. Thing is, I don't think we ever talked again, but I met many people who said he had balls and was a good leader.'

They reached the lift doors with the keys in their hands but changed their minds and ran up the stairs, a spontaneous and private experiment to find out who would be first.

Numa won.

On the Dance Floor

'On the other hand this one was a *clean war*, if there's anything like that,' said Eduardo.

Much water had passed under the bridge since the last time he and *Numa* had seen each other. They were catching up now, as they sailed a rented boat along the Uruguayan coast south of Colonia. On the starboard horizon a group of sails could be seen on their way to Buenos Aires across the river. They were probably racing, their spinnakers inflated like coloured balloons. Eduardo talked, reflecting on the war and comparing it to 1976.

'The coup was necessary, everybody was pretty fed up,' he said. 'The sixties ended in a mess. People wanted somebody to inject some order and complained we didn't have the balls to step in and save the country. I'm still convinced we were acting in defence of democracy, for we faced an international terrorist movement supported by Isabel's government.[*]

---

[*] Isabel Perón inherited the presidency following the death of her husband, Juan Perón. A weak and scantly learned woman, she had no previous experience in politics. Her administration was riddled with intrigue and corruption and she promptly delegated almost all decisions to her (formerly her husband's) minister of social welfare, José López Rega, who had no qualms about forming agreements with international terror leaders like Fidel Castro, Muhammar Gaddafi and Yasser Arafat. As a result of his deals, terrorist organisations in Argentina experienced substantial growth and were able to acquire modern weapons and military equipment.

'But then our own untidiness became visible as we started doing things that had nothing to do with soldiering. The Navy was split. Massera[*] had his loyals who were mostly corrupt and virtually untouchable. You had to watch your ass, for he had snoops everywhere.

'Illegality became the norm, the budget was a joke and COs were expected to make do with what they had. There was a lot of petty crime going on, though very few got richer. From this perspective the Malvinas was a fantastic opportunity to stop the decline. Aside from that, you know me enough. I never cared for the Islands. But I had my orders and nobody had forced me to enter the Navy.'

It wasn't the first time Eduardo had talked in this way. They had discussed these things extensively while on the Islands. Like his friend, *Numa* felt he had joined more out of a sense of duty than of patriotism. In April '82 he was having the time of his life in Angra dos Reis, scuba diving with friends. As soon as he learned of the invasion he returned to Argentina, for he was after all an Ensign in the Naval Reserves.

He showed up at the Navy's HQ. But they thanked him for his eagerness and sent him home unceremoniously, so he kept pestering them until he got his orders. Luck had him arriving in Puerto Argentino,[†]

---

[*] Admiral Emilio Eduardo Massera was the Navy's most senior officer and its leader. A devious and heartless opportunist, he had a Machiavellian mind and enormous charisma. He claimed the personal allegiance of a group of high-ranking officers which was unofficially referred to as the 'Personal Friends Group'. In the same way that Perón had done as the head of his political party and then with the national administration, within the Navy Massera's wish ruled, regardless of the law.
[†] The Argentine name for Stanley.

frozen numb after having flown over in the hold of a
Hercules transport aircraft dressed in his summer
whites, the one uniform he kept. There he found
Eduardo standing on the tarmac.

Eduardo was happily surprised when he saw him. He
had no idea that his friend had decided to join once
again. Taking advantage of the fact that *Numa* had a set
of very vague orders he introduced him to his boss, a
short and moustachio'd Captain from the Marines, and
suggested that he be assigned to his own platoon.

The Captain gave *Numa* an intent look and
congratulated him for his eagerness to fight for the
Fatherland. He was somehow fervent, and one could
hear the conviction in his voice. After briefly looking at
Numa's papers he accepted Eduardo's proposal and
dismissed them both, not before telling *Numa* that his
duty was to help win the war but, most importantly, to
return alive, for there was still a lot back home that
needed to be done in order to bring the country to where
it ought to be. At this *Numa* could not help feeling a
mixture of pride and respect for the guy, for it was clear
he was prepared to die there if necessary.

Eduardo's section consisted of a group of combat
divers[*] mixed up with a group of amphibious engineers.[†]
The assortment was odd but effective. Every man in the
group was an experienced professional soldier. Their
first days on the Islands were spent setting up minefields
designed by the Army engineers.

Mid-July found the section on Tumbledown. One

[*] Personnel belonging to the Agrupación de Buzos Tácticos
(Combat Divers), Argentine Naval Special Forces.
[†] Personnel belonging to the Compañía de Ingenieros
Anfibios, Argentine Marines.

evening they were moving to close a gap in the perimeter when they realised that the Brits had sneaked between them and the rest of the force.

They had no communications. They had exhausted all their batteries and the promised refreshments never arrived. It was night and Eduardo was considering a tactical retreat, for they had not made contact for over six hours now. The Brits kept pouring people behind his position and he did not want to be cut off from his main unit.

He knew he could do nothing but delay their advance and he had no objections to dying doing it. But the enemy was now moving rapidly south and he wanted to make his boss aware of this development, so he decided to send a messenger in the person of *Wizard* Quispe.

Carefully he emerged out of his foxhole and suddenly heard the sound of somebody crawling towards him. He had almost made out *Numa* when a mortar shell burst almost between them.

The blast stunned *Numa*. When he came to, Eduardo's upper body was projecting from the foxhole, his face buried on the peat. He crawled forward until he got to his friend and verified he was still breathing. Satisfied, he pushed Eduardo back into the foxhole and was about to return the way he had come. But he changed his mind and decided instead to check the foxhole on his right, where *Tony* and *Bear* were hiding. He knew in advance that *Bear* had been hit.

Tony was about to shoot the approaching shadow when the light from a nearby explosion allowed him a better look. *Numa* threw himself head first into the foxhole to learn that *Bear* had actually been wounded with a bayonet.

'Did you finish the guy?' asked *Numa*.

'God, no! You're such an animal!' answered *Bear* with a grin *Numa* did not see but could hear. 'But I didn't offer him tea!'

Numa stood up and got his head out alongside *Tony*'s. The firing had decreased, but now it was possible to hear British voices. They were coming from behind the position and they seemed to be growing fainter, but it was not easy to locate their source precisely. It was dark and they didn't have night-vision goggles. A well-aimed bullet had destroyed the last pair. It was not possible to make out anything during the flashes of distant explosions and for a moment he forgot himself, mesmerised by their effect against the darkness.

Each explosion and each burst lit up the landscape for a second or less in what resembled a movie made by a madman. *Numa*'s eyes retained each image in the same way he remembered having experienced strobes on the dance floor: an incoherent succession of snapshots.

It suddenly occurred to him that the enemy fire was slacking. The periods between gun-bursts were growing slightly longer. Summoning up strength he left his refuge and crawled back to Eduardo's foxhole. He arrived there almost at the same time as *Wizard*, who was coming from the opposite direction.

'How's it on your side?' he asked.

'I believe there's no one left,' answered *Wizard* coolly. 'I checked four foxholes and everybody's dead.'

Just then Eduardo decided to emerge from his foxhole and he did it with such liveliness that he almost knocked out *Numa* with the top of his helmet.

'What's up? What are you two doing here?' he asked anxiously. 'Where're the rest? *Wiz*, why are you here? What happens on your flank?'

'Think we're done, boss,' said Quispe.

Numa became suddenly aware that the sound of firearms had ceased around them. There was still very little light, colours were unclear, but now there was enough clarity to see. Eduardo crawled out of the foxhole and told them to search the perimeter, but before they had covered five metres he stood up straight.

'Lie down, don't be an asshole!' whispered *Numa*. Eduardo was silhouetted against the precarious light making an easy target for the most inexperienced of snipers, but no shot was heard. *Numa* too got up slowly onto his feet, wondering where had the Brits gone.

'We've been overrun,' said Eduardo aloud. 'Sons of bitches, they overran us!'

'What do you mean *they overran us*?' asked *Numa*.

'Can't you see?' asked Eduardo, almost shouting the question. 'We were run over, left behind, almost as if we had been another lamp post! We're cut off!'

Gradually *Numa* began to understand what had happened. The British attack had overrun the section's resistance and moved on ahead without realising that they were still there. Or perhaps they had realised and went along without caring?

Eduardo was furious. What *Numa* saw as an incredible piece of luck, his friend took as a personal affront. The idea that the Brits had overrun his position while leaving him alive offended his professional pride and made him question the decisions he had taken during the night.

Numa tried to talk him into the notion that the attackers had used the brief period when he had been knocked out during the shelling to run over the position without realising they were indeed still facing resistance. But Eduardo felt that the chance of doing his job had been snatched from him in the decisive moment of the fight.

They explored the position in the yet-undefined dawn expecting every moment to hear a shot that would take them out of the absurd situation they were in, until they were able to confirm what *Wizard* had announced. Aside from them, only *Tony* and *Bear* had been left alive. The rest of the section had died fighting, every single man had run out of ammunition long ago, and in several foxholes the fight had been at close quarters. Argentine and British soldiers were lying mixed up under the freezing haze, some with bayonets still gripped in now-rigid hands.

Without necessarily diminishing the friendship they shared, that morning affected Eduardo deeply and somehow changed the nature of his relationship with *Numa*. If until that point the officer had listened sympathetically to his friend's views about the Process* that he had lived from afar, and about the future of their country, thereafter he became less flexible and more demanding.

Something hardened inside him and their conversation became stiffer. The responsibility he had felt towards the section had been almost physical and, looking at his dead men, he knew he would never be able to forget what they had been through. His world had suddenly turned as black and white as the landscape against which he now stood with his companions, four solitary pieces on a forgotten chessboard.

---

* The reference is to the 'Proceso de Reorganización Nacional', as the military junta called the process they intended to fulfil while in power, and which was still held as their strategic goal at the beginning of the war.

The Zombies

It smelled burnt and he couldn't tell whether his eyes were open. The reek hurt in his throat and he felt he was falling from a great height.

He was really scared.

It occurred to him that maybe he could not see, so he raised his hands to his face. He couldn't see them.

He heard Elena's voice coming from very far away. He couldn't understand what she said. She babbled about lights and a hat standing at the entrance. And then she said something about a pair of boots.

'Why is she wearing boots?' he wondered. They were at the movies, nobody walked there. And what was all this fuss about the lights?

'Malvinas, Malvinas,' insisted Elena.

Had she gone mad?

The smell now was of damp earth, as the smell in Aunt Hilda's backyard where they used to play with the red-roofed wooden train with the shattered nest of a hornero bird. They climbed on the swing and jumped from it as if they were circus performers. They were super-heroes. It was hot.

'What's the matter with you?' he asked. 'What's that about the Malvinas?'

'Salinas! Salinas! Wake up, you idiot, they blasted us!' He heard the crackling voice of *Lanky* Antúnez.

'It went off just above the entrance. I can't find my boots. You have to help me find my boots! They pulped us, Salinas! Wake up, you son of a bitch!'

Suddenly he remembered where he was. He stopped

feeling like he was falling but he still couldn't see anything and for a moment clung to the image of Aunt Hilda's backyard, one corner full of empty bottles.

'Don't shout!' he said, not realising he was screaming. 'What boots? Where are we, *Lanky*?'

He still couldn't see and was suddenly paralysed by the horror of it. He was blind!

'Sergeant, sir!' he shouted desperately. 'Sergeant! Sir! Help me! Sergeant, sir! I can't see anything! I'm blind! Help me! Sergeant, sir!'

Again he heard Antúnez's voice: 'Shut up, sissy! You're a fucking clown!'

It smelled weird now, like burnt leather. He tried to move a hand and his arm wobbled out of control as if loose. He was falling again, but now the giddiness had turned into nausea. As he felt lighter he saw Elena's face again. Her pale braids were tied up with red ribbons.

He had already stopped caring when he heard Antúnez's voice once again. He was still trying to find his boots.

A push on the shoulder brought him back to reality and he heard a voice:

'Here, *Numa*! This one's also alive!'

He opened his eyes and saw a tired and dirty face. The man looked old.

'Can you hear me, soldier?' the face was saying, 'Can you hear me? Can you tell us how many you were?'

Another face appeared and he recognised the camouflaged uniforms. No-bullshit soldiers, he thought, and it took him few minutes to grasp what was happening. Everything around was covered in thick fog and he couldn't tell whether it was morning or afternoon. He could see the bodies lying among the stones, some of them in impossible positions.

He turned his head and saw Antúnez looking at him with eyes wide open. He didn't twitch a muscle. He seemed frozen. Without much surprise he understood that he was looking at a corpse and noticed that his partner had lost his legs from the knees down. He saw other people moving about.

'Fourteen,' he said, when he finally managed to find his voice. 'I think we were fourteen.'

Unable to hold it, he began to cry.

'Fourteen,' repeated the man, jotting the number in a little notebook. 'The bomb probably went off right above you, because here we found only nine. Aside from you, that is. All in all we make ten.'

He bit his lip.

'But some bad luck, for fuck's sake! It must have been a ranging shot. This sector was shelled three days ago and should already be out of the bombing charts. No one thinks there are any troops lurking around here. Were you guys inside a tunnel?'

He didn't answer. He didn't know what to say. Something told him that he shouldn't have been there at all.

'Don't worry, we'll talk about it later,' said the man, and turned around. 'Can you walk?'

He got up slowly. He felt unsure. He had a swollen knee and both his legs felt like cotton. The man who had talked started walking, but after a few steps he stopped and turned, extending a hand that he shook without really reflecting on it.

'Mendoza. Lieutenant Eduardo Mendoza, combat divers.'

'Salinas,' he muttered, more confused than impressed. 'Recruit Javier Salinas.'

They walked for what seemed an eternity. They marched in silence, but he was so tired that he could only focus on surviving. He didn't understand what was happening and he didn't care. They tramped over the frozen peat and he followed with precision every step the Lieutenant took.

From time to time they would pause, a guy called *Numa* would kneel to point a compass, and then he would read a map.

It was darkening when they stopped for a rest and the Lieutenant talked to him for the first time since they had started to walk.

'Fourteen,' he said once more, looking intently at him. 'And tell me, Salinas, do you remember now a little more of what happened? We saw the explosion from about 500 metres and then heard shouts, so we got nearer. I already said that we found only nine of you, some in better shape than others. Well, ten including you. But where were the rest? It's hard to believe that we didn't see a trace of them. Another thing I can't understand is how we heard all that screaming when we found that only you and this one here were able to talk. By the way,' he said, pointing behind Javier, 'he still seems to be on another planet.'

Javier turned to look to where the Lieutenant pointed and realised that throughout the march he had preceded two men who carried a stretcher.

He approached them and recognised the wretch as Ricardes. Half of his face had turned into a chunk of coal criss-crossed with streaks that oozed a sticky liquid. The right arm had disappeared from the elbow down and the tip of one of his boots pointed in an awkward direction. Javier leaned toward the face and felt the stench of burned flesh.

'Kid! Ricardes!' he called slowly.

The boy's single eyelid closed to reopen and the gesture filled Javier with sorrow. 'Ricardes,' he thought bitterly. 'The group's youngest, the best looking one, who surely had had more girlfriends than any and seemed to have been born to win them all!' Now he was ruined, his face disgusting and almost grotesque.

'A friend?' asked Mendoza.

Without premeditation but unable to control himself, Javier turned and started shouting, 'You shit! You sons of bitches, you murderous fucking shit!' as he tried to reach Mendoza with his fists.

Mendoza took a step back and raised the machine gun that hung from his shoulder.

'Soldier!' shouted a voice, and Javier stopped as if hit by lightning. The guy they called *Numa* was training his gun on him.

'Soldier!' repeated *Numa*, without lowering the muzzle.

'It's okay, *Numa*!' said the Lieutenant. 'The kid's still half shaken, he'll soon be over it.'

Javier's knees gave and he collapsed by the stretcher, sobbing loudly.

They were now on what had until recently been the scene of fierce encounters between the British streaming from San Carlos and the Argentines defending the outmost perimeter positions.

Although his rescuers seldom spoke, Javier grasped that they were not at all happy with the development of the war. Listening to the two who toiled behind him with Ricardes' stretcher, he understood that the Brits had surrounded their entire platoon during a night combat and these five guys he saw were all that had been left. He also learned that they were combat divers, although he couldn't understand why they behaved like infantry.

He learned that they were trying to make contact with their main unit, even though it was clear even to him that they were now too far behind enemy lines, and they had run into Coronel's shelter as they were making a detour to get around the front.

Numa and Lieutenant Mendoza appeared to be in the lead. The other three were low profile and nimble. One was called Quispe but everyone else called him *Wizard*. Balbo, one of the stretcher-bearers, seemed to be quite at ease in that terrible place. He seemed to have enormous endurance. The other one was a huge man carrying a knotted handkerchief on his head as if in a pirate movie. They called him *Bear*.

He sat next to Ricardes and listened to his breathing. The night was pitch-black and he could hear *Bear* and Balbo speaking on the other side of the stretcher.

'We did right, we wouldn't have been able to take them along.'

'Anyway,' Balbo replied, 'it breaks your heart, poor bastards. Who knows who'll find them and what he'll do with such a load. But who could've been the cunt that decided to leave them there, by themselves? For all we know, the only rank there was a Sergeant's.'

As if waking up from a dream, Javier realised that they were talking about his section. Lieutenant Mendoza had told him that they had found nine, ten alive including him, and for the first time since they had started walking he reflected that only Ricardes and himself were there. What had happened to the others, where were they? Without hiding his surprise he asked aloud, 'Did we leave the rest over there?'

There was an awkward silence. Then he heard *Numa*'s voice. He was obviously somewhere close, but in the dark he had not seen him.

'It was the safest thing to do, both for us and for them. They were all stunned, they couldn't even understand when they were spoken to. The effect of the explosion will eventually go away and they'll find somebody or be found by someone who'll surely help them out, 'cause they are quite harmless.'

Steps approached.

'Try to recover some energy,' Quispe's voice said, as a couple of hard biscuits fell into his hand. 'It isn't a lot and they are mouldy, but it's better than nothing.'

He ate in silence, thinking how easily he was taking in things that yesterday he would have found intolerable. Confused and exhausted, he surrendered to the darkness and fell asleep almost immediately as the wind whistled wildly through the rocks he couldn't see.

The Desert

The desert seemed never to end. They had spent hours driving up the road that split the landscape into halves. *Numa* thought the whole place looked dull and empty. He had slept a little and now the dusk painted everything in a dim, indefinite, dismal light as the red sky to the west grew darker and darker.

Tony drove as in trance, his eyes fixed on the road. *Numa* felt his mate had full control and closed his eyes. Minutes after, or so it seemed, he was startled as one of the wheels slid onto the roadside, making the pick-up swing violently.

Calmly, *Tony* took his foot off the accelerator, as if the risk of tipping over was nothing to break sweat about. He then let the truck run a few metres before coming to a halt. He turned the contact key to the off position and stepped out on the gravel. There he threw his arms up and let out a big yawn.

'I'll take over,' said *Numa* from his seat. 'Just let me shake myself a bit. You must be completely done, you've been driving non-stop for nearly five hours!'

Tony didn't answer. He stood behind the truck with his body turned towards the sea none of them could see, even though in Patagonia the sea is always present: miles away from the coast you still tread on snail shells, fish bones and seagull feathers. And it smells like the sea. You may be in the middle of the desert, but it still smells like the sea.

He coughed and lit a cigarette.

Numa came out in the cold and ambled a bit. He kicked a few rocks off the road and immediately felt refreshed. He had the weird feeling of being in a place where time didn't matter, but nevertheless he checked his wristwatch and considered the distance yet to be covered. They had travelled for the last fourteen hours, stopping only to re-fuel from the gasoline drums they carried on the flatbed.

'Let's go!' he said, climbing behind the wheel and buckling his belt as *Tony* took his place, slamming the door.

'Bit of a shitty trip, don't you think?'

'Better sleep,' answered *Numa*. 'We still have a long way to go.'

He started the truck and drove as *Tony* catnapped at his side. He felt relaxed and kept his eyes fixed on the cone of the headlights as the miles went by monotonously. Suddenly he spotted the outline of a man's back along the left side of the road.

He slowed. The man seemed bent over but walked with good rhythm. He was almost level when he turned around and *Numa* saw that he probably was in his fifties. He lowered the window glass.

'Care for a lift? We seem to be going in the same direction,' he asked, slowing to a stop.

'Thanks, but no thanks!' said the man. 'I'm almost there now.' The voice was hoarse. It was obvious that he had drunk a bit.

Numa was about to insist when *Tony* mumbled whether they had arrived and immediately realised his error.

'Close the window,' he said. 'It's fucking cold out there!'

He was getting snug once more under the parka when he saw the face of the man in the window.

'Who's that?' he asked. The man remained silent.

'Hop in, chief!' insisted *Numa*, 'The night is cold.'

'Okay,' said the man, 'if you insist. I'll climb on the flatbed!'

'Fine with me,' said *Numa*. Past the beam of the headlights the night was as dark as a cave. 'But you are welcome in here if you'd rather be warm.'

'No, thank you!' insisted the man, offering him a weak smile. 'I'd rather ride on the back. I like the cold.'

He threw his duffle bag on the flatbed and climbed on nimbly. *Numa* closed the window and waited for the tap on the roof before giving gas. *Tony* was already snoring. After a while he heard a new tap and stopped. He heard his passenger stepping down and rolled down the window.

'We're here!' said the man.

Numa looked in the direction of the voice but could see nothing. Slowly his sight grew better and he was able to make out the man's shape against the blackness. To the East the dawn was still a murky glow and he couldn't see anything around that could serve as a mark to the place where they had stopped.

'Are you sure?' he asked.

'Yes, yes! It's right here!' replied the man. 'Just a little further and there I have my things, I do.'

Numa was convinced that the man was confused. There was no sign to be seen, there was a wind blowing, and the temperature was surely going to stay low for a while until the sun was done heating up the air.

'Listen here,' he said as gently as he could. 'It's none of my business, but I wouldn't recommend you to go searching for a place to stay out here in the middle of the night. I can get you to the next town or maybe to a farm shed, I just have to keep driving anyway. But here where we are there's nothing but stones and wind.'

'Don't you worry,' said the man, and for a moment *Numa* believed he saw a smile cross his face, but discarded the idea. He was tired and his eyes were playing tricks on him. 'I've been in Soledad* before. Just leave me here, I'll be all right.'

'As you please,' said *Numa*. 'But let me offer you something to drink at least, you may be thirsty.'

He turned to fetch some sodas from the bag resting at *Tony*'s feet but when he looked back out of the window the man had gone. 'Good luck!' he shouted into the darkness as he engaged the gear and accelerated, slowly, so as not to trouble *Tony*'s slumber. He then rolled the window up and concentrated on the road. The car radio was out of order and he began to whistle low as *Tony*'s head bobbed like a broken doll's under the parka.

He came to with a startle. He had hit something. It was still dark and the road ahead lay empty.

'Didn't you see it?' asked *Tony*.

'See what?'

'The sheep, you moron! You ran over it!'

'Holy shit!' said *Numa*, and stepped on the brake with such violence that *Tony*, who had not buckled up, struck the windscreen with his head.

'Stop, for God's sake!'

'That's exactly what I'm doing!' said *Numa*, getting out of the car. He could make out a shadow sitting on top of the road, some ten metres behind the truck. As he came closer he saw it was a ram. It was frightened and tried to get up on its legs but something had broken inside. *Numa* returned and pulled out a pistol from the glove compartment. Walking up to where the beast was

* Soledad (Loneliness) is the Argentine name for East Falkland.

lying, he fired the gun with the muzzle almost inside the animal's ear.

Tony approached.

'What d'you think? Should we take it with us?' he asked.

'Can't leave it here,' replied *Numa*. 'If we find a hut we'll put it there and give notice to the first person we meet.'

They resumed the trip with the carcass on the flatbed. *Tony* went back to sleep but *Numa* had awakened with the accident. It had reminded him of an episode on the Islands, when they had run into a bunch of confused conscripts.

A bomb or a mortar shell had fallen on top of the group as they were emerging from a sort of underground shelter they had been hiding in. When *Numa* and his buddies found them they were calling the names of their comrades, who were not there any more. He could still recall their stink, like soaked sheep's skin. It was the stench of filth.

They were eight, or so he remembered.

The recollection shocked him because it had been a long time since he had last thought about the war. In spite of it, this trip they were making was rooted in the Malvinas. It was an attempt to reunite a group of friends who had been there more than twenty years before, following an idea raised by *Bear* Contreras.

Numa had arrived in Patagonia six years before. He had raised some cash in Venezuela and set up a diving centre in Puerto Pirámides. There he rented out boats and diving gear and took tourists around the gulf on scuba and sightseeing trips.

Tony showed up two years after and opened a pizza joint. Shortly after he was selling more beer than pizza and a couple of months later he moved in with a German girl who owned a house by the sea and painted quite acceptable scenes of the local fauna. Between them they turned the pizza parlour into a trendy café that soon became the local divers' preferred watering hole and was on its way to becoming a landmark.

One evening when *Numa* was visiting, *Bear* showed up at their door. He was managing a ranch in Uruguay, was on his way to a meeting with ranch owners down south, and decided to drive all the way from Buenos Aires to enjoy the emptiness of Patagonian roads. He was going to Comodoro Rivadavia but somehow knew his friends were there and decided to drop by. He had a crate of champagne with him and they emptied half of it, remembering old times until he proposed the idea of getting the group together for a long weekend at his place in Uruguay. He wanted to discuss a project with them and wanted also to use the chance to show them around.

They needed to get hold of *Wizard* Quispe, who as far as he knew was living in Río Turbio. The latest news he had was already three years old and had *Wizard* as the owner of a hardware store or something like that, married and the father of two. *Numa* and *Tony* offered to make the trip for him and *Bear* gave them all the data he had.

There was little if any work along the gulf during the season and both could afford to take a few days off, so next afternoon *Tony*'s girlfriend fixed them a huge icebox with sandwiches, sodas and beer. After throwing together a few clothes in a pair of duffle bags, they hung two signs reading 'Out on holiday' and took off in *Numa*'s pick-up truck.

They didn't know it yet, but they were going to cross other tracks besides *Wizard*'s in the big desert.

The Red Bandana

Antenor Rueda was born in Granadero Baigorria, close to the bridge that leads to Victoria, on the other side of the river. He was thirteen when his mother died and the very next day he left the house where he had lived with seven younger brothers and which also doubled as their father's butcher's shop.

From then on he lived from hand to mouth around the cheesy hotels and bars of Rosario's lowly neighborhoods, taking menial jobs in exchange for a little food and a place to spend the night.

He had a restless mind, a somehow wobbly basic education, and a natural ability to learn fast. He spent most of his idle time reading whatever fell into his hands and, early in the mornings, while washing floors or setting the tables before the bars opened, he would listen with interest to the musings of the many tramps who showed up for a drink, the refugees from society who – like him – had fallen out of the system and were invisible to the rest of the people.

Lacking alternatives, he promptly embraced Communism, clutching this ideology with the intensity of a martyr on a mission.

He found a mentor in Eufemio Pereyra, whom everybody knew as *Lame*. Eufemio was twenty-two and the son of a union leader who had – according to him – been murdered by political opponents. To the police officers in charge of the investigation the untimely death of the union strongman had been an accident, it had been very dark on the scene and the bus that ran him over had been missing a headlight. In any case, not even the most sceptical among the witnesses could rule out the possibility that the driver may have had a drink too many, particularly because he had not realised that he had run someone over until a passenger told him. By then the bus was already half a block away from the spot.

In any case, to *Lame* and his friends the affair had every sign of a politically encouraged hit and even before the wake was over they had set fire to seven of the thirteen buses parked at the terminal. The ferocity of this speedy revenge, once the fire and the explosions of the fuel tanks awoke every neighbour in the vicinity, turned them into heroes for every delinquent in the area.

Nothing was left of the buses to salvage but the matter did not end there. Three days later the same band seized the guilty driver as he was leaving his home, dumped him in the back of a van and left him back on the same spot some hours later after working him over and smashing his knees with an iron pipe.

This was in 1969.

A year later and *Lame* had already made a name for himself, accompanied by a police record. In September 1970 he took part in the attack the PRT-ERP* carried out on the offices of the 24th police precinct, where two policemen were killed. Although he was still a newcomer to the criminal world and still quite young, his reputation grew fast and he had to leave Granadero

---

* PRT: Worker's Revolutionary Party, a Trotskyist organisation active during the '60s and '70s. ERP (People's Revolutionary Party) was founded in 1968. It would grow to be the most powerful rural terrorist organisation in the whole of South America. Both organisations were destroyed during the Junta's government after Roberto Mario Santucho, leader and commander of the ERP, was shot dead in July 1976.

Baigorria to avoid getting caught.

Enraged, the police began harassing his friends and it was soon clear that he was one of the most sought after criminals in the neighborhood. The butcher's shop closed after the police mistreated his father to induce him to reveal where Antenor was hiding. The poor man died within weeks, overpowered as much by his shame as by the beating he had received.

In 1972 Antenor found himself an active member of the FAR.* They were soon to be united with Montoneros, who had been growing significantly after a successful attack at La Calera.†

He was sixteen and to his friends he was known as *Cholo*. He lived in a hovel in Fuerte Apache,‡ then known as 'Rev. Mugica's Liberation' neighbourhood. Now he seldom met *Lame*, who was still operating with the ERP and had been one of the members of the 'Segundo Telésforo Gómez' command, which together with the FAR claimed responsibility for the assassination of General Juan Carlos Sánchez, commander of the 2nd Army Corps.§

Antenor was cautious and didn't trust anyone, which in those years was a good policy because the bullies of the DIPA (Division of Antidemocratic Police

---

* FAR: Revolutionary Armed Forces, an irregular armed organisation of Marxist-Leninist orientation, founded in the '60s. Its members were originally recruited from among the Young Communist Federation –the *Fede* – of the Argentine Communist Party. Their objective was to join the rural guerrillas organised by Che Guevara in neighbouring Bolivia.
† On 1 July 1970.
‡ A marginal, gang-infested neighbourhood in Buenos Aires.
§ On 10 April 1972.

Investigations) worked always in disguise and were loose throughout the city.

The murder squadrons of the Triple A* were soon to join them after Raúl Lastiri reached the presidency.

When he was not busy keeping on the run or planning small robberies to gain experience and renown, Antenor was looking for information and opportunities to be seen in meetings where people discussed the ideological foundations of violent action. While he didn't feel any need to justify the struggle against what he clearly saw as a regime of social injustice, he needed a model in which to believe, or perhaps just some sort of hope.

He would never forget 20 June 1973, National Flags' day. It was already three days since he had arrived in Ezeiza, having walked all the way from downtown with other sympathizers, and there they were, among thousands of other Perón followers, anxiously waiting for their leader.

With him was Yayi, a girl from Río Cuarto about his age. She was tiny and had auburn hair. She also had steel nerves and was a very good shot. Antenor had seen her in action once when they got rid of a guy who was double-crossing the Orga.† The man was sitting at a table in a bar talking with two cops in plain clothes when Yayi shot him from the window of a moving car, from about fifteen metres. The bullet had passed clean through the bloke's neck.

Antenor was also inside the bar, both to confirm the

---

* Triple A: Argentine Anti-communist Alliance, an extreme right-wing organisation that was especially active during Isabel Perón's tenure. Created in 1973 by her Welfare Minister José López Rega, it worked outside the margins of law, carrying out 'Death Squadron' style operations.
† Slang for Montoneros, the 'organisation'.

killing and finish the job if necessary. He saw the bloke's neck burst. The face fell on the coffee cup, breaking it and stained the tablecloth with a mix of blood and coffee, while the cops dived onto the floor and got out their pieces. She had held her cool and shot without shaking.

Then – God knows why – Yayi developed a soft spot for the skinny silent kid always looking for a way to stand out. That morning in Ezeiza* they had been going steady for three months already but had worked together only that one time. They carried out their affair with discretion, for sentimental relationships were not encouraged among committed fighters.

Antenor was exultant. The return of the General offered a great chance to set straight, for once and forever, the scores with the military. Onganía, Levingston and Lanusse† would pay for having oppressed the people and screwing up the country during their illegal tenure.

Every organisation that mattered was there and each intended to make itself heard. From early morning Ricchieri Avenue was a river of people, everybody wanting to reach the elevated platform that had been specially erected to receive the leader. The Philharmonic Orchestras of the city of Buenos Aires and the Colón Theatre were already there, along with the City's Symphonic Band, as was the Permanent Choir of the Colón Theatre. Leonardo Favio‡ had announced that he

* On 20th June 1973, Perón's followers gathered in the woods around Ezeiza, some 35 km from downtown Buenos Aires, to welcome him on his long awaited return. Official reports estimated the public attendance at 3.5 million people.
† Three former Argentine military dictators.
‡ Leonardo Favio (1938-2012), Argentine filmmaker, script-

would release eighteen thousand pigeons to greet the General's arrival, one thousand for each year of his exile.

Antenor toured the groups with Yayi, joining in the spontaneous chants of 'Perón, Evita, the Perónist homeland!' 'We can feel it, we can feel it, Evita is here!' and 'FAR and Montoneros, they are our comrades!' that arose here and there.

'One can breathe victory,' rejoiced a jubilant Yayi. The loudspeakers screamed popular folk songs, it was easy to feel more Argentine than ever before. Antenor believed they were at least four million people waiting for the Leader who was returning.

At noon the enthusiasm began to grow. Everybody was singing *Los muchachos Perónistas*,* and jumping to the rhythm. Then followed the choruses: 'If this is not the people, tell us who the people are!' and 'Argentina! Argentina!' Yayi's face was crimson with excitement. 'Look!' she said. 'It's the people's anger.'

The shooting broke out without warning and the people surrounding the platform hit the ground as if mowed with a scythe. Favio, lying flat on the floor of the shack from where the music was being pumped, called for order through a microphone. He asked for the pigeons to be freed and kept on asking for 'Peace, peace, peace!'

Antenor heard somebody cry, 'It is those ERP sons of bitches!' and at the same time he caught sight of a group running toward a clump of trees, shouting, 'Our lives for Perón!' and 'Perón, Evita, the Perónist homeland!' From within the trees, armed men were fending off the people

writer and singer-composer. A very active Perónist supporter, he had a major role in the party's propaganda establishment.
* The official anthem of the Perónist Party.

who looked for shelter by firing at them. Right beside him, another group was shouting, 'Bring them here and we will kill them!'

He was downright confused but did not lose his cool. This was not what he had expected and he realised with some amazement that he had never quite known what to expect.

He turned his head, trying to locate Yayi, but he couldn't see her anywhere. His attention was caught by the spectacle of a man being dragged onto the platform by his hair. Once up there they began kicking him viciously. There was a huge bloke jumping on top of his chest to the rhythm of the people's chants.

He started to realize that something had gone terribly wrong. He was pretty sure he had heard explosions and now there were even armed guys on helicopters flying over the area, though he heard someone say that the choppers had come only to evacuate the wounded.

Still there was no sign from the General.

'This is a disaster,' he thought, and started contemplating leaving.

He still couldn't locate Yayi and everybody around him seemed to be in utter panic. There were many wounded and everywhere he looked he saw confusion.

He started in a random direction, not really caring where his steps would take him. He just wanted out of there as soon as possible. The sun was setting as he came to a group of houses near the border of La Matanza district, when something among the willows that bordered a brook caught his attention.

He got closer carefully, unwillingly startling a bunch of kids that had gathered there to build a fire. The headlights of passing cars from the nearby motorway made it difficult to see, and he got nearer.

Something that looked like a bag hung from a low branch. Getting even closer, he noticed that it was the body of a dead man. It hung from a noose, as he had seen in westerns. It dangled almost half a metre from the dirt and a blue nylon rope around the neck forced the head to one side. This was covered with a black plastic bag and a piece of cardboard had been fastened at neck's height. It read 'Erpista'.

With a touch of gallows humour someone had crossed out the 'E' and replaced it with 'Ha'. Now the sign read 'Harpista'.

He turned his eyes to the highway. It was almost dark already but he could still make out the colossal amount of people spread out over the fields. Occasionally he could hear a rifle or a pistol being fired, and shouts of fear and pain would emerge from the background of chants and amid the beat of drums. He drifted aimlessly, outraged and scared.[*]

He returned to Rosario and tried to find *Lame*. He couldn't, it seemed as if the earth had swallowed him. He tried not to consider the possibility that the worst had happened, he trusted him to be too clever to get caught.

In September the Monta[†] murdered Rucci[‡] in what they later publicised as *Operation Traviata* in an allusion to the popular twenty-three holed cookie of the

---

[*] The official figures of the clash between different factions of the Perónist party known to historians as 'The Ezeiza Massacre' specified thirteen dead and three hundred and sixty-five wounded.

[†] Montoneros.

[‡] José Ignacio Rucci (1924-1973) had led the CGT, the powerful Argentine Worker's Union, since 1970. Politically very prominent, Perón had acknowledged him as his 'right hand'.

same name, for he was shot twenty-three times.

For the first time ever, Perón wept in public, saying 'They cut my legs off...'. It was all very confusing, and many believed that the CIA had had a hand in the murder.

Antenor's perspective grew narrower. He was a fugitive from his own frustrations. It dawned on him that perhaps the struggle for egalitarian ideals that *Lame* so vocally supported was turning him into an instrument for something very different from what he had imagined. *Lame* was an idealist, he concluded. The political struggle was something else.

Nevertheless, he was at Plaza de Mayo on May 1st when Perón expelled a column of Montoneros as they chanted 'If Evita were alive she'd be Montonera,' and accused them publicly of being 'infiltrated mercenaries'. He was there as one of the many who run along the marching column painting the word *Montoneros* on every flag and banner. He had to be careful for there were many police mixed among the people, looking for faces they knew. On the corner of Junín and Paraguay he had to run in order to avoid getting caught.

As Montoneros were exiting the square to the chant of 'Aserrín, aserrán, this is the people that's leaving!' he spied a group of kids jumping out from the newly smashed windows of a bakery on the Diagonal. Some of them carried big plastic bags they had stashed with stolen soft drinks and boxes of chocolate. As they ran by where he stood one offered him a couple of croissants that he ate, listening to the chorus from the column that was now moving up Corrientes avenue: 'Attention folks, attention folks! We have a mole inside, his name is Juan Perón!'

He spotted Yayi unexpectedly. She was almost

hidden inside a narrow entrance, leaning on the wall, and had a red bandana tied around her head as she talked to a tall thin guy in a leather jacket.

He was making his way towards them when Yayi turned her head. As she saw him she motioned him to approach and the guy on the jacket turned to look at him with unaffected interested. He had John Lennon-looking glasses and blond hair that was beginning to thin at the top.

Antenor had not seen Yayi since Ezeiza but knew that it was not smart to show they were intimate in the presence of a stranger, so he approached with a casual grin. Yayi's face betrayed nothing.

'This is Pablo,' she announced, shaking her head in the direction of the tall guy. 'He's just arrived from Tucumán, where they're preparing something big. I'm off with him this evening, would you like to come? We must keep on fighting for the cause and this here is already lost. We will try to do it from the inside instead, from where it is needed.'

Antenor thought that it was still possible. In Buenos Aires all the paths were closed. That same night they nicked a van and drove it off to Tucumán.

They arrived in Simoca at four-thirty in the afternoon and abandoned the truck in a vacant lot. Pablo had made stealing food an art, and during the trip they resupplied from the kiosks in the gas stations. He was a History teacher and had taught in a couple of rural schools in Córdoba.

He had joined the movement in '69 at the Cordobazo with Tosco,* and from there he had gone to Tucumán,

* On 29 March 1969, the city of Córdoba was paralysed by a

always hoping to help fight a war that he considered revolutionary, for the workers' benefit and fundamentally Socialist. According to him, the comrades had been working seriously in the region since last March and now the Mountain Company was almost ready.*

'It's only a matter of days now,' he said. 'The boys are eager to try themselves.'

Thanks to Pablo's skills as a provider, when they arrived in Simoca they still had plenty of food, so they split the leftovers before breaking up. Pablo was to join some comrades who were operating in the area, but Antenor and Yayi decided to keep on towards Monteros to get used to the region and try to locate another group which Yayi knew about. They parted without shaking hands. By now Antenor didn't care if Pablo and Yayi had started something together.

In any case, they never reached Monteros. They were walking on the side of a dirt road when a truck came speeding behind them. A crew of strangely dressed guys rode on the flatbed. As they went by, some of them pounded their fists on the driver's roof and shouted him to stop. They carried a variety of firearms and were dressed in what seemed to be old military fatigues.

Yayi and Antenor ran towards the truck that by now

popular protest raised against the dictatorship of General Juan C. Onganía. Agustín Tosco (1930-1975), union leader and a member of CGT leadership, played a prominent role in the uprising.
* The Mountain Company 'Ramón Rosa Giménez', created in 1972 in the mountain forests of southern Tucumán, is considered to have been the first organised cell of the ERP. It did not go operative until 1974.

was reversing. The driver was somehow untrained and almost ran them over, but when the truck finally stopped some of the guys in the back stretched their arms to help them climb. They all looked very young, somewhere in their late teens, and carried a messy assortment of weapons. One of them clung to a heavily adorned shotgun and when he realised that Antenor was eyeing it he proudly held it up, explaining that he had found it hanging on a wall in a summer house in Villa Nougués and thought it would be a pity to leave it there. Antenor nodded silently.

The truck drove past Monteros and the sugar factory of Santa Lucía before starting up the mountain by the ravine known as *de Los Sosa*. It was getting dark and they could see the lights of Famaillá and farther to the North the glow of San Miguel.

After a while they stopped and left the truck to continue on foot through a cattle path that penetrated a deep ravine. Yayi had been chatting with a boy who carried a regulation pistol on his belt. He said he was from Santa Fé and had come to take part in the appraisal and PR activities that accompanied the creation of the Mountain Company, led by *Red Head* Irurzun, though everyone there called him *Captain Santiago*. He had very blond hair and the other kids called him *Dry Grass*.[*]

They walked for a couple of hours more before turning into a smaller trail disguised by the thicket of tarcos[†] and vines, and night had fallen when they came

---

[*] 'Dry Grass', and later 'Captain Raúl', were war monikers used by Lionel McDonald, last leader of the Mountain Company. The events here described have no relation at all with the actual person.
[†] Local name for the jacaranda tree.

to a clearing surrounded by two sheds made up of fallen tree trunks and roofed with leafy branches.

In a corner, a Primus stove heated a rough iron kettle.

Soon Antenor would have his first taste of *huascha locro*,* Years later, he would look back fondly on these days.

They would leave the campsite early, after a round of *maté*† around the fire. They followed narrow cattle trails branching to distant roads that led to previously chosen settlements where they would carry out their mission of indoctrination. They never went the same route twice, and every now and then they used the truck to travel between distant villages. There they spread their message among the underprivileged dwellers, laying the ground ready for the day when the Central Committee would decide to go into action. It was said that the Party's intention was to declare the whole province a liberated zone.

People were normally friendly and the visitors were often welcome to *maté* rounds, but it was clear that they did not care much about revolutionary theory. Antenor and his comrades spent most of the time helping in common tasks and preaching the idea of social justice in the best way they knew, threatening small merchants who refused to cooperate and distributing the products of big-scale robbery practised by better-organised factions upon major producers. Not knowing better, the folk received these goods as if they were gifts from the

* Hot stew made of corn grains and other greens, typical in north Argentina.
† Infusion normally drunk from a gourd through a metal straw. Members of a '*rueda de mate*' sip in turns.

sky and were grateful to the youngsters that showed such generosity.

On 30 May 1974, the ERP made its triumphal entry into Acheral flying its emblem, a red star emblazoned over the blue and white stripes of the Argentine flag. Antenor was there with Yayi and precisely on the same date the Mountain Company 'Ramón Rosa Jiménez' began to operate its armed wing,

Those were days of glory. He felt he was living the genesis of a new nation in the same fashion someone had told him that a guy called John Reed had experienced in Soviet Russia. His relationship with Yayi was cooling fast but he was not particularly worried, for his days were filled with chores he felt deepened his personal search. The distraction of a romantic relation wouldn't help this process.

Some of the kids were fond of reading and one lent him a copy of Mao's Red Book from where he stole phrases he used to improve his proselytizing arguments.

The party came to an end on 11 August when the Mountain Company was hit while preparing the takeover of an Army Regiment in Catamarca province. Only four guerrillas managed to escape the ambush and sixteen were executed by firing squad in Capilla del Rosario. This setback was especially painful for Antenor, for among the fallen was one of the few persons he had ever cared for: *Lame* had died true to his ideals, which so many in this world seemed to be against.

On hearing the details of the bloodbath, Antenor suddenly felt exposed. With *Lame* gone, the source of his revolutionary zeal was reduced to the memory of a few coffee-laden nights when he had heard his friend quote from Mao, Gramsci, Marcuse and other authors he himself had never heard of until then. He would probably never read them, though their words had then sounded like the true Gospel.

Someone had told him once that History is written by the winners, and that made him think bitterly that probably nobody else but him would ever remember the courage and the commitment he had seen in *Lame*. Disappointed, he decided to return to Buenos Aires. He didn't even tell the others, he didn't care whether he was found and executed for his desertion. 'And in any case,' he thought, 'life's just crap.' ERP was not his cup of tea and although he wouldn't have been able to put it into words, he felt that his interest in Marxism was more intellectual than operational.

He left on his own. Yayi remained with *Dry grass* and would be with him until the end, when he was killed already under his identity of *Captain Raúl*. Shortly before that, on 1 July, Perón died and his death precipitated the fall.

Operation Independence[*] smashed the tactical organisation in Tucumán and months later, in Monte Chingolo, the last hope of the ERP[†] died. Nevertheless,

---

[*] Operation Independence was the campaign organised by the Army to put an end to the guerrilla warfare in the mountains of Tucumán. It answered to a Decree from Congress (No. 261/75) issued during the elected government of Dr Italo Luder. The Decree commanded the Army to 'proceed to implement all the military actions deemed necessary to the neutralisation or annihilation of all activities of subversive factions in the province of Tucumán'.

[†] On 23 December 1975, ERP attacked with over 150 guerrillas the gun depot of the *Domingo Viejobueno* Battalion in Monte Chingolo. The attack was successfully repelled and the official account mentioned about six military and one hundred civilians dead, of which only forty five of the latter were effectively identified. This was the last operation worthy of mention carried out by the organisation.

the fight went on for several months, as both sides were bent on destroying the opponent.

In mid-1976 the whole country was under military control and the Orga collapsed. Through the influence of a Rosario man who had known his dad, a skipper turned owner of flat-bottom pontoons that carried sand and other goods down the river, Antenor got hired as a deck hand on a barge that shuttled fruit and wood between Quilmes and Puerto Garibaldi, on the banks of the Uruguay River.

He wanted to have a place of his own, so he found a cheap room in the back of a hotel in Quilmes. He had a view of the river and in the afternoons he would watch the putrid banks of water lilies slowly float by with their hidden cargo of bullfrogs, spiders and snakes.

He would often take long walks when ashore. They took him into the surrounding neighborhoods and soon he got used to the narrow sidewalks of Villa Dominico. He liked his loneliness and ended up renting a bigger room at a boarding house, in Sarandí. When in the mood he would drop by the brothels of Avellaneda, which would remind him of similar joints he had patronised as a teenager in Granadero Baigorria.

Sometimes he would cross the bridge over the Riachuelo to ramble for hours in the city proper, hands in his pockets and a cigarette dangling from his lips. He would walk up to Caballito and spend the siesta feeding crumbs to the pigeons on a square, or reading the news at a table in some little café in Mataderos.

One December afternoon he was enjoying a grappa at the Oviedo when he was handed a Montonero's pamphlet. In addition to the usual harangues, it carried the news that the Orga had executed three deserters a few days previously, forcing them to jump from the eighth floor of a building in Rosario. The account didn't give names or aliases but included a badly printed picture of the offenders. Despite the poor quality of the image he was able to tell Yayi blindfolded, still wearing her red bandana.

Antenor was a survivor and he knew it. Often, when on the boat, he would chat with *Tachito* and Rodrigo, the two other sailors. They were much younger than him but were also more experienced on board. *Tachito* was the only son of Don Pedro, the skipper. He had been sailing the river since he was a child and could read the water like no one else.

Under Don Pedro's watchful eye, Antenor learned quickly and soon became a skilled hand on deck, it was as if he had never done anything but sailing the river.

Tachito helped him to study and he stood the tests needed to obtain a Seaman's licence. In the process he realised that he loved the job. He even took another exam and got licensed as a Naval Motorist, which gave him some of what most people would have defined as professional pride.

He had buried the combatant. He felt that with Perón gone the Montonero's cause had dwindled into an even darker confusion of individual-driven aims and personal revenges that did nothing to bring closer the goals the party proclaimed.

His interest in politics waned steadily and before he knew it his life reached a stability it had never had before. At times he would miss the excitement of the former days and wonder if he too had ended up charmed by the despicable blandness of middle-class life. Eventually, he came to think it didn't really matter, because we only live once and – even more important – for a very short time.

The Malvinas War broke out in April 1982 and found Antenor sailing up the river. Hearing the news, every boat on view began to blow its whistle and hoist colourful flags as the crews gathered on the decks to hail each other and celebrate the re-taking of the Islands. Some even lit their emergency flares and brandished them from the bridges as if it were Christmas, and the VHFs were jammed with mutual congratulations. God was Argentine once more.

The following week they summoned *Tachito* to the Regiment where he had finished his military service eight months before. Don Pedro was heartbroken.

'What the hell do we have to do in this war?' he asked nobody in particular. 'Don't we have enough professional soldiers in this country? Why is it that they need to call in also those who have already done their time?'

Antenor could see that there was probably logic in calling in trained troops if the country was going to fight a war, but could not help sympathising with the old man. He was also convinced that the military were only good to screw the people and therefore suspected that the retaking of the Malvinas was nothing other than a sorry attempt to make everybody forgive them for the past six years.

Soon the war was on everybody's mind. People everywhere talked about the Malvinas, Thatcher and how Argentina was going to fuck the English in the ass. Antenor felt his fighting instinct coming back. Seizing the opportunity to level his debt with Don Pedro, he announced that he would join. In that way he could be close to *Tachito* and make sure that he returned safe.

The old man almost wept his thanks at this proposal but added that he would be happier if he stayed on the boat because his leaving would force him to reduce the frequency of the trips, and anyway the chances of him finding *Tachito* among all the soldiers that were being deployed were very slim.

But Antenor's will was not so easy to overcome. The more he thought about his plan, the more excited he felt about facing combat and experiencing once again the adrenalin rush he now realised he had been longing for.

Taking advantage of a day when Don Pedro was feeling low, he persuaded him to believe that everything showed the war would be so short that there was no reason to worry about it, that at most he would have to skip two trips with the boat, but that on the other hand they would win significantly in the appreciation of their clients for having collaborated so unselfishly with the cause.

As for his chances of finding *Tachito*, he said that he knew people in the Army who could easily shuffle the soldier's billets so as to make sure that he and his son would be together. The whole thing was a blatant lie, but the old man believed him and so the following day Antenor showed up at the local recruitment office. To his surprise, they took him in without any further questioning.

He arrived in the Malvinas on 26 April as the driver of a Colonel's jeep, but after waiting two hours on the tarmac for someone to tell him where to go and pick his vehicle he decided to take advantage of the too apparent disorder and disappear from Puerto Argentino.

Without even caring to hide his movements, he crossed the landing strip and kept walking towards a ridge that rose in the distance. In addition to his backpack he carried a bag stuffed with canned food and water bottles. He had a number of combat rations and a

FAL with three full clips. The perimeter sentries stopped him twice but he addressed them briskly and said that he was in haste to comply with very important and classified orders, adding for good measure a sardonic comment on whether they thought him so thick as to try to leave his unit just like that in plain view of everybody. The sentries were just kids. It proved easy to deceive them and they let him go.

His plan was to survive and – given the chance – kill British soldiers, for the Islands were Argentine and it was time to teach those sons of bitches that they had no business down there. Though he didn't know where or when it would happen, he was pretty sure that sooner or later he was bound to make contact with Argentine troops, and then he would need a credible story. However, for the time being he expected to be left alone.

On the fourth day of his trek he found a cave in the slopes of Rivadavia Mountain and decided to use it.

It was close to the summit and he disguised its entrance using stones and peat. From there he could see the houses of Fitzroy from above. He didn't know the place's name but at night, to the east, he could sometimes see the horizon lighting in the direction of Puerto Argentino.

On 1 May he woke to the sound of Royal Navy gunfire and soon after listened to the sound of helicopters flying to the west of his position. He didn't have the slightest idea of how the war was turning out, but he could see people moving among the houses and near the bridge.

He hid for three days more, listening to the flight of helicopters and fighter planes over the cave and then to the Harriers' attacks on Darwin and Puerto Argentino. Then he decided it was time to leave. He wanted to travel light so he built a pile in a corner with the food he didn't need, thinking that even in the case that he didn't return there would be others who would eventually make good use of it. When night fell, he climbed to the summit and then turned north, in direction of Mount Simon.

He walked slowly, careful not to make noise. The night was cold and the stars shone against a jet-black sky in which the moon had not yet appeared. He could guess the profile of the mountain ahead and decided to turn slightly west to circle its summit while keeping on the slope, thus passing between the dark boulder and the coast.

He had no maps, but something told him that he was far away from heavily-patrolled areas. He changed course again and began plodding his way northwards. The cuffs of his parka were dripping in the cold drizzle and soon he lost all notion of time.

He walked, engaged in his thoughts, and must have relaxed his attention, because the *Clack!* of a bolt being slammed took him completely by surprise. He hit the ground as if touched by lightning. He couldn't see anything and the only thing he heard was his own breathing. He was lying with his belly on the dirt. As he struggled to remove his backpack while making the least possible noise he felt a colossal weight falling on top of him and a strong hand buried his face in the peat.

He then felt the hand pulling his helmet backwards in an attempt to choke him with the chinstrap. Milling his arms around like crazy, he managed to lift his face from the bog while not quite succeeding in turning his body upside down.

'Son of a bloody b-!' he said and had to cut it dry, for just then the attacker released his grip on the helmet and at the same time the weight was lifted from his back. He scrambled to his feet with the gun still in his hand and tried to locate the aggressor in the dark, but it was impossible to see anything.

'You're an Argentine!' he heard someone say behind him, as if speaking from a height.

'Of course I'm Argentine, you motherfucker!' he answered furious, turning around. Nothing. He couldn't see anything.

'I almost killed you!' said the voice, a little closer this time. 'I am sorry, I couldn't see you clearly!'

Now he could see something, a smudge in the dark.

'Who are you?' asked the voice. Antenor was prepared. He had had time to decide that the best approach to interrogation would be to fight it back with questions. In addition, the fact that this guy was addressing him so informally told him immediately that he was in front of a draftee and therefore he did not have much to worry about.

'None of your business,' he said. 'Who are you?'

'Martín,' said the voice. 'Martín Cañizares. Are you lost?'

Antenor did not answer right away, he wanted first to know what ground he was treading on.

'Are you here alone?' he asked.

'No,' replied Cañizares. 'We are a group of sorts, we lost our Lieutenant and we are now waiting here. A Sergeant is in command. We are hidden, but I came out because I was dying to take a leak.'

It was the chance Antenor expected, handed on a platter, he thought, to rejoin without hassle or uncomfortable questions. The lack of an officer in the group was an almost unbelievable stroke of luck. Officers always asked too many questions and they wanted to know, they distrusted as a norm.

The Sergeant that this rookie was talking about would

be far easier to convince than any brass, and he had
nothing to lose by giving it a try.

'Cool!' he said approaching the shadow. 'Let's go and
see your Sergeant then!'

They walked a few metres until they reached what
looked like a pile of large rocks. Adjusting his eyes to the
light of the moon that now loomed from behind the
clouds, Antenor thought that if those stones were the
hiding place the kid talked about he could have come up
with a far better one.

Cañizares advanced and asked him to wait for he
would warn the others that he was not returning alone.
Then he disappeared among the boulders. There had not
gone two minutes before Antenor could see the
silhouette of a man perched on small height yonder
signalling him to approach.

He climbed his way through the rocks until he was
face to face with Sergeant Coronel.

Antenor joined the group and decided to stay as long as
it was comfortable. He could certainly use the company
and they all seemed to be good kids. Some were more
mature than others, but all had a youthful playfulness
that reminded him of old times.

The Sergeant was also a good guy, although he had no
fucking idea of how to manage people. He was scared
shitless and you could tell it. The conscripts were simply
desperate, but like all kids they would vent it out talking
nonsense and exchanging crazy stories.

As a newcomer who was considerably older that the
rest of the group, it was easy for him to make up a
credible story in which he had been the only unharmed
survivor in a reconnaissance patrol and introduced
himself as Corporal (1st Class) D'Amico.

The Sergeant, a short dude with the face of a Quechua indian, did not ask for more and once Antenor learned that he was dealing with an army clerk he stopped worrying about the credibility of his story. 'The dude has no idea of where the fuck he's standing,' he thought, and forgot about the problem. To his amusement he soon discovered that everybody there, including Coronel, held him in high respect. For some reason they seemed to believe that he knew better about that war they had been thrust into and didn't dare to question him.

In consideration of his declared condition as professional military, Coronel granted him unusual privileges and sometimes went so far as to consult his opinions.

He kept his distance by playing mysterious, and was allowed to leave the shelter in expeditions of capricious length without having to explain to anybody where he had been or what he had done.

One night he left for one of his walks some hours after the area had been intensely bombed. He just couldn't stand any more sitting idly inside a stinking hole, no matter how big it may have been. 'I have to move over,' he said to himself, 'if I really want to see some action in this war.' With luck, he thought, he may even find his way to the unit to which *Tachito* had been assigned and which in all probability had already been deployed.

But he didn't want to sneak away like a robber, he had come to like some of the kids and it would have been wrong to leave as if he didn't care what would become of them. Some of the youngsters were full of questions and others were convinced that they had seen it all and had nothing else to expect from life, but somehow they all had hope and he felt he couldn't fail them.

He wandered over the frozen peat in direction to the

cave where the group was hiding when he heard the sound of distant shooting that made him thank his lucky stars once more.

A shadow shifted in the distance in front of him, right at the entrance of the pit and before he knew it an appalling explosion threw him to the ground, blinding him momentarily and leaving him breathless.

He was sure that he had stepped on a mine, but despite the desperation borne from his momentary blindness and with his eardrums almost burst, he managed to check with his hands whether he was at least still in one piece. He tried to rise and found he could not stand. The air he was desperately trying to get in had the taste of burnt cordite and he thought he heard screams.

He recovered gradually and realised that something had exploded just a few metres in front of him, precisely at the mouth of the refuge. Moving awkwardly, his balance lost, he came upon a human torso that still had a head attached and recognised it as Vergara's, one of the recruits. Overriding the shock and fighting his revulsion, he crawled in direction of the cries under the dim light preceding dawn.

Moving still at ground level, he raised his head and saw what was left of the body of Sergeant Coronel lying beside two other bodies that were apparently complete. Feeling a pang of nausea he rolled over to lie on his back.

He couldn't believe he was alive. Once again he checked his body as thoroughly as he could, carefully feeling each limb and dreading to find an unpleasant surprise at any moment.

He found nothing.

He was whole.

Slowly, and straining not to lose control over his movements, he rose to his knees and kept rising until he stood up, still a little hunched, but at least on his own feet.

Everything he could see was covered in a thick fog, or so it seemed. The screams had ceased now and he could only hear some muted groans. Someone nearby was reciting the Lord's prayer but suddenly the voice died in the middle of a phrase and he didn't hear it again.

He lingered a while, without knowing very well what to do. He tried walking but every step brought back unbearable nausea and his legs felt as if they weighed a ton.

Presently he heard distinct voices, they spoke Spanish and somebody was running. Partly instinctively and partly because he was unable to do anything else, he let himself fall behind a rock. Now he could see them well.

It was an Argentine patrol. One of the soldiers was talking to a wounded conscript. They all wore camouflage, which told him that most likely they belonged to the Special Forces. Without knowing very well why, he considered that he would not be able to explain his being there in an acceptable way. He was the only one in the group who had not been injured.

'These are serious professionals', he thought. War for these men was not a game and they were not there just to play soldier. He would not be able to deceive them.

Without thinking twice, he was gripped by the panic of being interrogated and found a deserter. Probably they would have him shot after finding out his real name and would make his cowardice and humiliating death into an example to other would-be deserters. To be exposed and remembered as a coward. He didn't want to end like that. He began to crawl away until he was at a good distance from the newcomers and hid under a huge boulder. Once there he turned to look back and knew that nobody would see him. Then, summoning all his strength, he stood up and started to run.

When Argentina surrendered Antenor joined one of the groups of disheartened soldiers who returned to the continent aboard HMS *Canberra* and landed at Puerto Madryn along with three thousand other ex-combatants, every one a shadow of what they had been just a few months before.

While on the boat he had searched tirelessly for someone who could offer news of *Tachito*, waiting anxiously before every gesture of doubt, before every wilful effort to remember.

He was finally able to run into a 1st Sergeant who had been in the same platoon with *Tachito*. He was dead, the 1st Sergeant said. He had died in one of the first Harrier attacks, while digging a trench west of the airport. A bomb. No corpse had ever been found, but *Tachito* and three other conscripts who were digging on that spot never re-appeared. Judging by the size and location of the bomb craters, it had been clear that none of them could have escaped alive. Two days after the attack, a group of conscripts found a shovel and a pair of right-foot boots in one of the craters. They still had the feet inside.

On their arrival in Madryn the Army returned part of his equipment, but he did not know where to go. As he had done so many times before, he just started walking without a defined purpose. Following the coastline, within a few days he found a wooden hut on the beach, and not far from it a little brook that ended in the sand. The hut was hardly a shelter. It was certainly abandoned and nearly destroyed. He thought it probably had been used as a shepherd's shack.

He had not eaten for two days and had very little water in his canteen. He found a large unlabelled tin in a corner of the hut. It was badly dented but otherwise unopened. He worked at it with his knife and saw it contained lard. It was rancid. It had probably been sitting there for years. He ate a little until revulsion beat him. Then he made fire with a few sticks he had gathered and lay down to sleep.

Time passed and he soon got used to his isolation. At the beginning hunger was a problem, but he was able to catch some seagulls that he roasted at once to make them last longer. He enjoyed loneliness and knowing that he was far away from everything. He decided that he did not trust people and felt he needed nobody.

Using the remains of a fruit crate and a length of rope that he found among the flotsam he managed to build a cage with which to fish crabs. He would load it with stones and nests of seagulls and other debris, then carry it into the sea until the waves reached his chest and drop it there letting it sink to the bottom. Then he would get back to the shack and wait, securing the device by the rope to a stake he drove into the sand. After a short while, he would always find some crabs inside it.

He got to know the area and carried out some expeditions, but he always returned to the cabin. Sometimes he would take longer tours that could last for weeks. These he would use to look for chances to make a little cash by taking odd, menial jobs that would not imply continuity he was far from wanting. He used the cash to buy canned food and kerosene with which he fed an old camping burner he had found abandoned on the beach.

Everywhere he went he would introduce himself as a

veteran, which was fairly easy to believe because the faded green uniform was the only garment he used when he was away from the shack. Sometimes people gave him money, other times they would pay him with old clothes or food. When he thought he had enough he would disappear again without leaving any kind of contact reference behind and went back to the shack, the gulls and the sound of the waves hitting on the beach.

Slowly he improved his living quarters, covering the openings on the walls with canvas and pieces of cardboard, adding a mattress, a table and a couple of plastic crates on which he sat to eat his meals.

Every now and then he would buy cheap, second-hand books, which he spent hours reading under the light of a fire or of the kerosene lamp. He felt a warm excitement every time he spied the lights of a ship sailing near the coast.

Except for those he met during his tours, he never saw anybody. He felt content living with his memories and weaved every kind of story with them, mixing elements, so that already he couldn't tell whether they had been real or imagined.

In all those years, the past returned to visit him in the flesh only once. One night when he was walking along a road, a pick-up truck stopped beside him and the driver offered to give him a lift. It was late and he was returning to the shack from Caleta Olivia. He had appeased his needs with a couple of gins and a Paraguayan girl with whom he had lingered a little too long. The driver did not realize it but Antenor recognised him immediately, thinking with a little bitterness that, as with *Lame*, probably nobody remembered him.

Anyway, he was through with people. This guy whom he could have recognised anywhere probably didn't even remember that episode on the Islands. But that night Antenor could not resist the temptation to remind him, so he told him that he also had been, once, in Soledad.

Back in his shack Antenor watched the waves dance, as the afternoon sky grew darker and darker. A few seagulls were flying in circles, chasing each other in that aimless game of theirs, and one darted suddenly upwards as if it were a dark blue arrow. He followed it with his eyes, feeling the sea salt rough on his lips. He closed his eyes and thought: 'Yayi...'

On the Road

Once again we were driving along roads that seemed to be endless. *Tony* drove and I thought about Indian raids and how hard it must have been to survive the desert then. I had fallen asleep without even realising it, shortly after leaving San Julián. From then on the landscape grows calmer, the slopes start to disappear and soon one is in the middle of the desert, where it seems that nothing ever happens.

Even San Julián has a feeling close to desolation, a sadness that not even the sea manages to wash away. The moment I woke up, *Tony* gave me a tired look suggesting I took over.

It was a wonderful morning, not a cloud in the sky. I took the wheel and after driving for a while I saw a large line of trucks parked, blocking the road straight ahead. They stood there like a mammoth caterpillar, and I stopped the pick-up some distance behind the last.

I could see they had already been a good time sitting there, for several *maté* rounds had already started on the roadside and nobody seemed very rushed. The sun was now quite high but the air was cold and there was frost on the road. I stepped down, took a few steps and stood rubbing my hands together to warm them. The whole scene looked like a Patagonian postcard and one could even make out the Andes in the distance. They looked almost translucent.

'Tipped!' the voice made me turn around. The driver of the truck in front of us approached, smiling. I checked its plates: SA. 'Salta,' I thought.

'A big double-trailer,' he said. 'Caught by the wind and went on its side, then bellied-up. The two drivers came out in one piece. They say it looks as if a big hand has put it on the road, like this,' he explained with a gesture. 'They are now emptying it to see if they can move it, because the roadside is too high and it won't be possible to pass it on the side.'

'We'll have to wait,' I said without much interest.

I was not intending to strike up a conversation, but he was not impressed by my short answer.

'Had a tough night?' he asked, tipping his head, which was round and flat, to the side.

He was being nice and I was being rude.

'No, sorry! Just a little cold.'

'Kettle's almost ready,' he said, 'and there are still some buns. Can I tempt you?'

It was too much. I looked inside the cabin to see how *Tony*, still asleep, stretched to take better advantage of the place I had left free.

'Don't need to ask twice!' I answered.

We climbed on his truck, a huge, brand new, bright blue MAN. The cabin was ample and really clean. The *salteño* was clearly a neat guy.

'You travel alone?' I asked.

'Y'know,' he answered, 'An old bull is better by himself! I've made this trip many times. I take it easy and enjoy it. The freight is never too urgent.'

He pulled a dark metal-rimmed *maté* out of the glove compartment.

'Bitter?' he asked and I nodded. I liked the guy. There was something rock-solid in the way he did things and the way he spoke. 'But so is it often with *salteños*,' I thought. 'Composed, solemn.'

'You come all the way from up there, from Salta?' I asked while he poured boiling water in the *maté*.

'I come from Jujuy,' he answered, stirring the yerba with a decorated silver straw. 'I am *jujeño* but the gentleman is right, I come from Salta.'

He handed me the *maté*.

'It's none of my business, of course,' I said, taking it and nodding my thanks, 'but do you mind telling me what are you carrying?'

'Timber. From Tartagal.'

He turned around and got out a few buns that looked like they were freshly baked.

'It's planks and finished boards I carry. We're going to build a school.'

I thanked him and took one of the buns. It was warm.

'I travel with my own portable oven,' he laughed. 'I dip the buns in water and put them under the hood, next to the radiator. In a little time they're as good as newly baked.'

'They are very good,' I said without lying. 'Is it the municipality that's going to build this school?'

'No. It is the neighbours. We have been waiting for the municipality to build it for five years already and now we've got tired. Now we will do it.'

'And the grounds?' I asked. 'And all the materials? Who pays?'

'We do. The neighbours,' he said, stretching out a hand.

'Oh, pardon!' I said, handing him the *maté* that I'd been holding as if it were glued to my hand. 'But isn't that a lot of money?'

'There aren't many other things on which to spend it around there,' he said smiling, 'and besides, we really need a new school.'

We ate in silence. The bun was delicious and as I ate I realised how hungry I was. Suddenly I remembered the dead sheep we were carrying on the flatbed. Although it was nothing to brag about, the man seemed so decent that I told him right away about the accident and asked him what he would have done in my place.

'It happens quite often,' he said. 'Don't fret, it's a common thing. A pity that you guys didn't skin it last night, now and with the cold it's going to be difficult. You could have done it in three minutes. Did you cut it open or is it still whole?'

'Whole,' I said.

'Mmm, I don't know.' He shook his head, as if doubting success. 'You'll have to leave it on the roadside, there's not much else you can do now. A pity.'

He felt silent as he offered me the *maté* once again.

'Nice truck!' I said, after taking a long drag.

'Brand new. We bought it three months ago.'

'Is it also the neighbours'?' I asked.

'No. This belongs to the *Tata*, it's one of *Tata*'s trucks. He has three in total.'

'Ahhh!' said I, as if understanding. 'Does he own a fleet?'

'Yes, but sometimes he rents them. He likes to take care of them, work on the engines. He believes he can fix them to work better. Now he wants to sell the Bedford and buy one of these new Mercedes. We're going to go pick it up together, he says.'

At that moment the door opened and *Tony* showed up, grinning.

'Hi there!' he hailed. 'It's damned hopeless trying to sleep in the car without the engine running, it's fucking cold!'

He climbed into the cockpit and closed the door.

'By your leave,' he said, pushing me aside to make himself comfortable as he stretched out his hand to my new acquaintance.

'*Tony* Balbo, it's a pleasure. I apologize for the inconvenience, but I was freezing.'

My host shook hands and squinted his eyes, studying *Tony*'s face. For a moment I thought that *Tony*'s lack of manners had angered him and got ready to say something in the way of apology, but without releasing the hand he was holding he asked *Tony*: 'Have we not met before?'

'I don't think we have,' replied *Tony*.

'I'm quite sure that I have seen your face before,' insisted the *jujeño* and added his name: 'Damián Lucena.'

'Lucena,' I thought while he offered the *maté* to *Tony*. 'Damián Lucena.' The name didn't tell me anything. I had known *Tony* for more than twenty years already and it would have been a surprise if these two knew each other from before.

Tony had few friends and I had never heard him mention a Damián Lucena. The only friend I knew he had whom I never met was a bloke who had been lost when the A.R.A. *Belgrano* sank. They had been buddies since they entered the Navy and a while later *Tony* had chosen the divers his friend had preferred to stay on board where he later had become a weapons specialist.

We kept the *maté* going around for a while, enjoying the break and talking about nothing in particular until we heard the other trucks start and I decided it was time to get back to our pick-up.

As I was climbing down from the truck's cabin the *jujeño* grabbed my shoulder.

'Are you going to skin that carcass?' he asked, 'or will

you just leave it on the roadside as it is? Because if that's what you intend to do I know of others who could make good use of it. It's a hard life out here and many people are in need almost constantly.'

'No problem!' I said. 'We were going to throw it away, but if we can put it to a good use, so much the better.'

I felt I was doing a good deed, for before I was done talking I could already see his features lighting up.

'I won't bother you with details,' he said, letting go of my shoulder, 'but I thank you very much. I know of a family who lives around here and will be all too happy to have it. She's a widow with two children, they feel this is their place in the world and don't want to leave, in spite of the fact that we have approached her with several offers to move and settle at least closer to town. But she won't! Her late husband was also from around here. Virasoro. He died in the Malvinas. I met him there. Small world, isn't it?'

Lucena had an honest smile and now he regaled me with one that was pure openness and which included – I thought – something that could be fondness.

'It was also there that I met your friend,' he said, alluding to *Tony*, who now inspected the wheels of the truck a few metres from us. 'He doesn't remember me but I recognised him immediately. I have a great memory for faces.'

'In the Malvinas?' I asked unable to hide my surprise. 'It can't be possible,' I added without stopping. 'I was with him there and I don't remember you. And we were always together, from the very beginning.'

'Nevertheless,' he insisted, still smiling. 'So it is! I don't remember you either, but him I do. War does strange things to people.'

The trucks were beginning to move, the column

looked like a huge snake crawling over the dry pampas.

'I'll bring your sheep!' I said, stepping down onto the ground and heading for the pick-up.

Tony and I lifted the carcass out from the flatbed and taking advantage of the distance that separated us from the *jujeño*, I asked him whether he knew him from before.

'No,' he said. 'Why d'you ask?'

We were now too close to Lucena, who was busy untying a corner of the canvas for us to throw the dead animal into the trailer.

'I'll tell you later,' I said. We swung the carcass and threw it in the trailer while Lucena held the canvas open. It fell with a thud. It probably weighed over 50 kilos.

Lucena gave us another big smile and held out his hand.

'We'll soon meet again, I'm sure!' he said to me. 'God brings together those he likes!'

Then he faced *Tony*, who stood next to the truck. Holding his hand for a moment he looked squarely at him, still smiling.

'You don't remember me now, but it'll come back. There are things one doesn't forget. We'll also meet again.' He dropped *Tony*'s hand with a warm shake.

'Drive safely!' he said, his arm raised in salute as he climbed onto the truck and started the engine. *Tony* and I were already heading towards the pick-up.

'As soon as I sat behind the wheel I was shocked by the contrast of our cab with the truck's, where we had enjoyed a few *matés* and buns that I now regretted not having saved for the trip. Compared with ours, it had looked as clean as a hospital ward. Ours looked like a pigsty. You could smell the stink of God knows how many cigarette butts mingled with the stench of half-finished beer cans, the floor was strewn with bread crusts and pieces of salami that we had shared the previous night. The reek of the clothes we had carried on for almost a day now completed the picture.

I eyed *Tony*, trying to look serious.

'You're a pig,' I said. 'You have to learn to live clean, not in this mess. This looks like a sow's bed.'

Tony was used to my anger fits, my variable obsession with order. He smiled without turning his head.

'It's really nice out there,' he said. 'You can walk a while. I've heard that it may turn you into a better person.'

We arrived in Río Turbio after sunset.

I had been there once in 1973 and what I saw then confirmed the expectations I had about a border mining town, where it was not unusual for people to resort to brawls or gunfights in order to solve their issues.

I am sort of fond of those kinds of places. It is as if folk who live in them understand that nothing is forever and that everything in life has a cost. So they learn to squeeze joy out of a landscape that is fairly depressing, even if you are an optimist. It's a quiet, hard life.

We drove by a hotel called *The Black Cat*. I remembered the name but in my memory it had belonged to a whorehouse. If I wasn't mistaken, it had surely changed for the better.

The town was larger now, but it still held its borderline character. This was the South as I remembered it, with wide streets silent but for the noise of the wind or some truck passing by. The days here were short.

I parked the truck in front of the first joint that seemed to offer coffee. I had been hours at the wheel and

I was not looking forward to leaving the car's seat for the cold of the street. I woke up *Tony* and he realised how groggy I was as soon as he opened his eyes.

'Wake up!' he said. 'Let's grab a bite and then we are going to find the *Wizard*. That's why we came here.'

He was right, of course. I opened the door and stepped out into Río Turbio.

Time Machine

They had arrived at the address that *Bear* had given them but there was no hardware store there. The road died on the closed iron gates of a huge depot.

They got out of the pick-up and peered through the gap that opened between the gates. They could make out a few wooden pallets stacked in a corner beside a stack of galvanized roof sheets that gleamed as if fairly new. Otherwise the place looked empty.

They were returning to the truck when a large trailer turned the corner and stopped with a big snuffle from its brakes. The cabin door opened and, as the driver stepped down, *Numa* raised a hand as a signal for *Tony* to let him handle what was coming, and stepped forward to meet the man.

He was still walking as the man's boots touched the ground. He carried his hair long under a baseball cap and his stubble was beginning to silver.

'Excuse me sir!' began *Numa* politely. 'Could you please tell me where...?'

He never finished the question. Instead, his lips parted into a wide grin as he spread his arms wide to embrace *Wizard* Quispe, whose face he had recognised under the cap.

'My dear *Wizard*!' he exclaimed. 'Still looking as mean as a ferret!'

Wizard smiled, perfect teeth in the dark flat face.

'And what are you doing here?' He asked, looking over *Numa*'s shoulder and towards the pick-up. 'What, isn't that *Tony* Balbo?'

The question sounded even more probing in his singing *salteño* parlance.

'And what've you both come to do here?'

Wizard was originally from Salta. His family belonged to the Aymara tribe. *Numa* remembered once he had confided to him, almost reticently, that he belonged to a lineage of princes. One night when both were sharing sentry duty during an exercise long before the war, he had heard him tell the story of the nation that was already ancient when the Spaniards arrived. *Wizard* saw the world through other eyes. He had the patience of a mummy and a face that seemed carved in *quebracho.**

He was a terrific cook but had never mentioned his ability, which was discovered by his mates out of pure chance during a stomp along the Negro River. They were eating around the campfire and *Opa* Mederos helped himself to the hare stew that was cooking in a pot. Before he did, and thinking that everyone had taken their share, *Wizard* threw some herbs in the mix to increase its taste before plunging his spoon to take the rest. Mederos had not yet helped himself and so he partook of the new concoction.

'But this is delicious, che!' Said Mederos, who was from Córdoba. 'What's that that you added?'

'It's just some grass,' answered *Wizard* without giving it any importance.

'But it changes the thing completely!' Insisted Mederos, now addressing the rest of the guys. 'This is the best stew ever!'

The same hare stew had been their diet for the last

---

* Schinopsis balansae. Very hard wood typical of the Argentine Chaco.

three days and everybody in the group was really fed up with it.

'Let me see,' said Quispe, taking a spoonful from Somoza's plate beside him. He tasted it and made an exaggerated face of disgust.

'And you guys eat this shit?'

Thereafter he was appointed official Chef and it was common to see him stop in the middle of a hike, grab a handful of herbs and put it in his pockets. Over time they found out that among the plants he gathered for cooking there were some he also used to prepare simple medicines. It was because of this that he came to be known by the whole unit as *Wizard*, despite the misgivings of some medical officers who sometimes supplemented the unit when in manoeuvres.

Now he was smiling as he slapped *Numa*'s shoulders with emotion.

'To see you again! That's why we came!' said *Tony*, approaching and hugging *Wizard*'s shoulders.

'What for?' asked *Wizard* raising his eyebrows. 'Don't tell me you guys miss me!'

'Just every now and then,' answered *Numa* with affection for the little man with whom he had shared so many adventures and whose calmness had reassured him so many times. 'I'm gonna tell you the truth, it would have never crossed our minds to come and visit you here, you know how lazy we are. But *Bear* dropped by Pirámides a few days ago and asked whether we could locate you because he's eager to get us all together once more, I don't know exactly what for.'

'Isn't he in Uruguay, *Bear*? Someone told me that he was managing a ranch there or something like that,' said *Wizard*, lifting a hand to his cap.

'Yes,' replied *Tony*, 'that's almost right. As it is, he

inherited some land there and is turning it productive. He's bought cows and everything, the fool has turned into a farmer!'

'And you two plan to stay a while with us, right?' asked *Wizard*. 'I'll fix you right away and you'll see what a great time we're going to have together. You guys come just in time to lend a hand in building our school. We started working a few days ago and we need all the people who are willing to help finishing it! How long are you willing to stay?'

Numa looked at *Tony*, who returned his gaze blankly.

'We were thinking... perhaps a few days,' said *Tony*, unsure about committing.

'Let's say that you'll stay until you're fed up,' said *Wizard*. 'We'll be happy to have you for as long as you wish to stay. Are you guys on your own?' he asked, looking towards the pick-up.

'It's us and our souls,' answered *Numa*. 'Us and our dirt.'

'Let's see,' said *Wizard*. 'We'll park your truck here in this depot by my trailer to begin with and then we'll go to the house. I'll introduce you to the family and we'll have some *matés* before we eat. That okay?'

'Beats it, dude!' said *Tony*, who, to *Numa*'s surprise, had suddenly adopted the colourful vocabulary of an outlaw. 'We can well dig some chow!'

Numa stood watching as his old partner climbed back in the trailer's cabin. Despite the fact that a lot of time had passed since they had seen each other, he felt it as if it had been just yesterday. *Tony* opened the depot's gates to let them drive in and after they parked the vehicles they walked around the building and crossed the few metres that separated the depot from the house, followed by the racket of the wind on the iron sheets of the depot's roof.

Surrounded by roughly finished cement terraces, the house was only one storey high, but the unevenness of the ground had forced the floors of the different rooms to be built at a different level. This made the whole building seem to have vertical development and thus it appeared lighter than other houses in sight.

Annie, *Wizard*'s wife, greeted them at the door. She was a redhead with a friendly and fully freckled face. 'Thirty-six or thirty-seven years old,' thought *Numa*. *Wizard* made the introductions.

'This is my Annie,' he said. 'We married in '84.'

'Pleasure!' said *Numa*, shaking Annie's hand, and *Tony* followed through. 'We are really sorry for showing up like this, without any warning. We hope it's not troubling you.'

'It's no trouble at all!' replied Annie shaking her red locks. 'Friends are always welcome here! Come in and make yourselves at home, you're probably tired after the road!'

After lunch they sat to have another *maté* round. *Tony* followed with interest the conversation between *Numa* and *Wizard* that was peppered as usual with memories and anecdotes, as he sat stroking Cachi, the house's dog that had immediately grown fond of him.

Now they were recalling a series of manoeuvres the unit had carried out in San José Gulf in '78, when the country's relations with Chile were still quite close. At that time, unlike Numa and *Bear*, *Tony* was a newcomer. 'A different tour and a different time,' he thought as he got nearer to the table to busy himself cleaning the *maté*.

It was during one of those exercises – when he was still quite raw – that he realised how easy it was to die in that job. The workday had ended and they were shooting the breeze inside the shop of A.R.A. *Irigoyen*, the vessel the Navy used to support diving operations.

They were waiting for chow time. Everybody wanted to make it an early night because next day's manoeuvres were scheduled to start about four in the morning, shortly before the low tide. Lieutenant Arrieta, head of the group, appeared at the door and told *Deaf* Antúnez that the aircraft carrier had reported a problem on one of the sea valves located close to the keel. She was anchored three miles off and the diving team had received the order to check it before sunset.

The Lieutenant thought that just a couple of divers would suffice to carry out the task properly, but saw no reason to relax the standard safety procedures to spare efforts. The party would consist of five divers and he would be in charge.

'We leave in twenty minutes,' he said, before running off to get himself ready. Presently *Numa* showed up. He had been on deck, changing a worn-out gasket on a coupling of the portable decompression chamber. He had also heard the order and told *Deaf* that he didn't need to sweat with this one. He was still wearing his neoprene and ready to go. 'You can easily stay here, you're probably quite done for after today.'

'I'm also in,' said *Wizard*.

'Thank you *Numa*,' Deaf said, 'but I'll be going anyway. I'm the oldest non-commissioned officer and I will definitely not stay here waiting for you guys to come back. But if you want to be one of the divers, it's okay with me.'

'You,' he said looking at *Tony*, 'you come with me and we'll be the second couple, okay?'

They left the shop to get dressed. *Tony* didn't relish

sitting in the boat with *Deaf* and the Lieutenant while the other two had fun in the water, but he understood it was preferable to have those with more experience take the first dive and locate the failure. *Wizard* and *Numa* had more diving hours between them than he could even begin to imagine. Also, those were his orders.

There was already little light when they approached the side of the aircraft carrier, a grey enormity that looked as if it was going to fall on them at any moment. Lieutenant Arrieta insisted that the divers carry a safety line, and this proved providential, because what followed gave rise to an exhaustive investigation in which each of the participants had to declare his version of events.

As it was, *Tony*'s statement was not very extensive. The only odd thing those on the boat had noticed was that after a while the diver's lifeline began to pay with increasing speed and ever more urgently until it reached its end. From then on it began to tow the Zodiac along the carrier's side in the direction of her stern until it sat almost on top of the propellers.

Once there, *Wizard* and *Numa* emerged with their faces congested, sharing a single air bottle of which the reserve valve had already been pulled.

But now *Tony* remembered it had been a close call and asked *Wizard* to tell the story once again.

'Do you still remember that?' asked *Wizard*, slightly perplexed. 'Of course,' he reacted, 'it happened during that period too! I remember that at the beginning of the dive everything was going well, we got in the water and nose-dived slowly, it was very cold.'

'Dead cold,' interrupted *Numa*, accepting the *maté* that *Tony* presented him.

'We got past the hull fin and continued towards the

keel, where it was absolutely black, so I felt for a welding seam to follow with the fingers to make sure we'd be able to find our way back in the darkness,' remembered *Wizard*. 'It was getting darker rather fast, but it was still possible to make out the sand on the bottom. We had covered about fifteen metres or so, and we were well under the hull when I lost the seam. I let off some bubbles to find the slope towards the sides, but it didn't help. The hull had a very flat bottom and the air stuck against it, leaving little pools upside down. We turned, looking around trying to find any glimpse of light, and it was then that I touched the bottom with my swimming fins. I thought it was a bit weird, for at the start of the dive the bottom had not been that close to the hull.

'It was impossible to communicate with this one,' he said, indicating *Numa* with a head movement, 'because with all the sand we had stirred and the almost blackness we were in, I could not see anything. My fingers finally found a seam and though I couldn't know if it was the same I had used before I decided to stick to it, for I didn't have any other reference. Mind you, it was easier said than done. The hull was very dirty and the water was so cold that my fingers had almost lost their feeling.

'It was then that this animal,' he said, pointing again to *Numa*, who nodded as if he were enjoying the memory, 'grabbed my hand and pulled it to his throat. Almost at the same time he snatched the regulator from my mouth and I realised that there was something wrong with his equipment. A moment later he returned it and I took some air before giving it back to him. From then on we took turns at breathing.'

He took a break to grab the fresh *maté* that *Tony* had reloaded.

'It was some shitty afternoon, really,' he said,

laughing, and looked towards *Numa*. 'I don't know how you remember it yourself, but you have heard me say that at that point I honestly thought we were screwed, since we could not see anything, we had a single valve and were lost under the largest hull of the fleet.

'So I began to draw on the lifeline as we took turns with the valve. After a while I noticed that there was some resistance and that calmed me enough, but it was still pitch-dark and it was clear that the hull was now much closer to the bottom.

'Suddenly I saw the faintest line of greenish light and I thought I was dreaming. It was barely visible, but I figured that *Numa* was watching the same thing and when I got closer I bumped my head against the hull. The lifeline disappeared into the line of light, the tide was ebbing and we were trapped between the hull and the bottom. We were enclosed by the edges of the bed that the ship had carved in the mud, every time it sat on the bottom at low water, after almost a week at anchor on the same place.

'I think both of us realised it at the same time, for we just started digging like crazy. It proved useless, for the sand on the sides filled immediately the gaps we were trying to dig. We tried to stop one of the corners from collapsing by using *Numa*'s bottle as a support, but we ended up losing it. The only chance we had was to swim along the green line and hope for the best.'

'I followed him,' said *Numa* to *Tony*, 'but I admit that I had given up already and didn't know if he had realised it.'

'I did imagine something like that had happened,' said *Wizard*, 'but preferred not to think about it. The damned lifeline was very taut and held our progress back. I was tempted to cut it. But it was the only thing that could indicate our position if we stayed down, for we were already too far away from the place where we had dived. I never thought we were going to drown, but had the feeling that *Numa* here was taking more and more time between breaths and a couple of times I thought he was done for. But it was clear that the son of a bitch had good lungs.

'At a certain point I began to make out the bottom again. We swam, almost scraping the hull clean, and I knew that if I could see clearer it was because we had more light. It had to be coming from somewhere, so I turned my head and saw that the green strip was no longer green but had turned light blue and was also wider. And so we were able to surface.

'As we swam up *Numa* handed me the regulator. I blew into it to dislodge the water and then sucked, but the air didn't come. I threw the reserve lever but it had already been thrown when I bumped it against the hull. We climbed slowly. I remember that I thought how stupid it would be to kill ourselves with an air embolism.

'I do not know if you remember,' he said, looking back to *Numa*, 'but when we got to the surface the Lieutenant threw a fit because we had not been able to find the fucking valve. He even said he wanted us to go back...'

'So many good memories', thought *Tony*. It had been fun with the divers.

Hearing them, it seemed that his friends had lunched together yesterday. As if time had stopped when the friendship and trust they shared was born. As if nothing had changed since.

It was almost twenty years since they had seen each other, and yet each silence, each gesture and each pun fitted seamlessly in their conversation. 'There are just some things like this, which do not die,' he thought.

'And if that's what you get from life, then it's more than enough for me.'

New Challenges, Old Memories

Wizard had left the Navy almost at the same time as *Numa*. By then he had already met Annie, the redhead from Dolavon whose Irish parents were the family's second generation in Patagonia.

He met her on his way to a diving competition in Puerto Madryn. He had been driving alone when, just a few kilometres from his goal, the van died on him. Fortunately there was a car driving just behind him and, on seeing his trouble, they offered him a lift that he gladly accepted, for he was keen on arriving well in time. Annie's dad was at the wheel and her mother sat beside him, so he climbed on the back seat beside Annie and they got on right away. In hindsight he thought that in spite of the awkward circumstances he had managed it pretty well when he invited the group to come and watch the competition. They accepted cheerfully and spent the whole morning on the jetty, following the event and chatting with the divers. That night they invited him to dinner and it was there that he ended up falling for Annie.

It hadn't been too soon. After having spent long time drifting he was keen to settle. A few months before, driving a truck bound to Río Turbio, he had spotted a warehouse for sale on the outskirts of town. It was large and solid, and the town was on its way to become a proper city. He liked it and he had a business in mind, but he first needed someone to settle down with.

They married shortly after the diving competition. Soon, with the help of Annie's parents, they bought the warehouse and moved to Río Turbio.

Business was good. *Wizard* was true to his commitments, tidy with his book-keeping, and soon earned the trust of customers and suppliers. He bought a piece of land adjoining the depot and erected a new warehouse.

One Sunday morning, luck rang his doorbell. When he opened, still half-dressed and just out of the shower, a local journalist, a microphone and a television camera were there to greet him. The journalist asked him how it felt to be the sole winner of the provincial lottery. Slightly annoyed for the interruption and a little confused (he didn't remember having played, for the ticket was Annie's) he only managed to ask 'Are you pulling my leg?' The interview appeared on every screen in the state and he became instantly famous.

At last he was able to make his plans real. He bought two used trucks from an oil company that was shutting down operations nearby and used them to deliver the elements he sold out of the warehouses. At first he worked alone. Annie was pregnant and she managed the office when he was not in town. He was never gone for very long, but there was a surge in construction and it was a busy life.

One evening as he was returning from a trip to Monte Aymond, he offered a lift to a man walking by the road. After they had talked a little the man said he was from Corrientes. He had headed south two years before for he felt Patagonia, with all those open ranges, fitted him better. Since then he had travelled most of it, done odd jobs in several ranches and learned different trades as he went.

Wizard told him he had been in Corrientes on a few occasions and had only good memories from them.

Then, thinking that he could well make use of an additional driver, he asked him whether he had any intentions of staying around. The fellow considered the question and eventually shook his head negatively. 'Too cold to be alone,' he answered.

They arrived at Río Turbio when it was already dark. *Wizard* had arranged to deliver a load of Portland cement to the owner of a pizza joint called *El Rebenque* and decided to drive directly to the place. It was still open.

Once the bags were downloaded, the man from Corrientes suggested they take a bite. *Wizard* accepted. He was hungry after all the driving. They sat at one of the tables and were about to order when the *correntino* spied an acquaintance among the customers and greeted him with a wave of his arm.

'That guy over there,' he said, getting closer to *Wizard*, 'is Damian Lucena, a *jujeño* with whom I've worked before. He is a good man. He'll do if you need a partner. He is a horse-breaker, but there aren't a lot of ponies around here and he seems to like the place. I know he's been on the lookout for a job for a while now.'

Introductions were made and the rest was easy. Both being Northerners in Patagonia, it didn't take long for Lucena and *Wizard* to find common ground. The man from Jujuy turned out to be hard-working and tactful, qualities that *Wizard* appreciated and which soon won the horse- breaker a position in the business.

They didn't have a lot of expenses – both *Wizard* and Lucena were of the frugal type – and the little firm grew. Annie got pregnant again, this time with twins. With most of the depot management in the hands of his new partner, *Wizard* focused on transportation, borrowed aggressively from banks and purchased another two trucks.

Only two months after the buy, currency devaluation – the type of those that only happen in Argentina – had almost completely dissolved the debt he had with the Bank. As if this had not been enough luck, Lucena's foresight meant that the warehouses were stacked with goods at the beginning of the predictable shortage, all paid for and ready for sale.

Wizard hired two local drivers but was not happy with them. He felt they were not entirely dependable. One Sunday while he was wandering with Annie in Los Coihues he ran again into the man from Corrientes. The guy – his name was Jorge Orcande – seemed happy to meet again and announced he had changed his mind and was now considering staying in Río Turbio. He had found a girlfriend since, and wanted to settle and start a family. Without thinking about it twice, and trustful that a friend of Lucena would hardly disappoint him, *Wizard* offered him job as a driver. Orcande accepted right away.

One year later he was married and had a son. *Wizard* offered him a plot of land as a wedding gift, close to where his house was, and there Orcande erected a prefabricated house in which to live with his family.

Wizard also helped Lucena to buy a house. The three of them got along famously. Between them they installed a fire system in both warehouses, and then the *Wizard* decided to buy some new trucks.

It was around that time, some three years before *Numa* and *Tony*'s visit – and while they sat roasting a lamb on the patio behind the house – that Lucena mentioned the Malvinas for the first time. He mentioned it in passing. He was actually telling them about a widow who lived with her children on a little shack on the slopes of the hill of the Vega Mala.

'I try to drop by their place every time I'm nearby,' he told them, 'in case they need something. They're very poor.' The first time he had seen them was when he spotted a pair of young boys at the side of the road and they motioned him to stop. They needed some kerosene and had brought a jerry can with them. He didn't carry kerosene in the trailer, but they filled the can with diesel from the spare tanks and then they invited him to some *matés* at their place. He accepted without mistrust, and as they neared the hut the widow came out from under the striped poncho that served as door. She was still young, with a service gun slung from her belt. Damián recognised the pistol immediately. But he played it as if he had not seen anything, and addressed her with courtesy while inwardly regretting his recklessness.

The woman invited him in and, on entering, he was surprised by the neatness of the place. It had a dirt floor which had been swept recently, and the few possessions on sight were neatly arranged. The room was almost filled by a rugged table made out of a large door and a wooden crucifix hung from the wall over a portrait opposite the entrance. The widow took a *maté* from a shelf and removed the gun from her belt with a swift movement, setting it on the table with the barrel pointing towards a corner of the room. 'Excuse the gun,' she explained, 'one never knows what to expect and my kids are too young to distrust.'

Lucena had nodded, smiling.

'Everything you see here was built by my husband,' said the woman, pointing at the portrait.

Lucena looked again at the picture. It was the photograph of a young man wearing a conscript's uniform. Surprised, he took a step closer.

'Is this your husband?' he asked, staring more

carefully at the picture.

'Yes,' answered the woman, moving closer to the gun now. 'He was killed in the Malvinas. Why?'

'Was his name Virasoro?'

That afternoon Damián Lucena spent a long time talking with the widow and her children. Carlos Virasoro had been one of the members of his platoon in the Malvinas and he had not made it back, having died in an explosion.

Damián remembered little of him. They had not had a very close relationship. But he remembered the young man's face as if he had seen him yesterday. There, facing Carlos' young widow and the twins he never got to meet, he felt overwhelmed by colossal grief.

'Hey, I never knew you had been in the war!' said *Wizard* when he heard the story.

'A very private man, this *jujeño*!' said Orcande, sucking on the *maté*'s straw.

'Just briefly,' said Damián. 'Briefly, but enough for me. We didn't get to fight but we were very scared anyway. They took us prisoner and we ended up in one of those concentration centres, as they called them. It was all very sad and coming back was really depressing, but at least we were alive unlike poor Virasoro.'

'And what exactly did happen to Virasoro? Were you there when it happened? Didn't you just say that you didn't see combat?' asked *Wizard* as Cachi approached, wagging its tail.

'Well,' said Damian somewhat peevishly, 'we were in a cave in the ground, so we saw nothing. There was combat, for sure. But it was happening in the open. When we came out the fight had ended.'

'And this Virasoro guy, where does he come in?' asked Orcande, who had shifted from *maté* to red wine, offering a round as the *jujeño* spoke.

'Virasoro was with us, that I have already said,' said Damián. 'It all happened as we were leaving the shelter, just as we came out. It must have been a bomb or something similar what fell very close and killed some of our party. Among the dead was Virasoro. Those of us who survived stayed there for a while but we were totally zonked, moving about like idiots. Then a group of Argentine soldiers appeared out of the blue and wanted to carry us with them, but most of us couldn't even walk straight, so they ended taking a couple, one who could walk and another on a stretcher because he was very badly hurt. The rest of us stayed there until the Brits showed up.'

'They left you there?' asked Orcande, unable to believe his ears. 'On your own? What shits! Sorry!' He put his hand to his mouth the moment he saw Christian, *Wizard*'s youngest son, leaning on his father's leg.

'Well,' said Damián, 'they had no other solution, really. It was like trying to herd a bunch of dumb cows. We were as deaf as lamp-posts and some of us couldn't even see. Some of us took almost two days to recover, but by then the Brits had already found us.'

They were quiet for a while, and suddenly *Wizard* said: 'It was us.'

'Who were us?' asked Lucena, freezing as he tried to slice a piece of the roast without getting burned.

'Us,' repeated *Wizard*. 'We were five divers, but we were there operating as Special Forces. We were on our way to the front when we found you. You were fourteen, or at least that is how I remember it. Five of you were dead. The rest were like babies or stunned cows, as you just said. We had arrangements to make contact and we couldn't wait for these guys to recover. It had happened as you are telling it, a bomb had fallen on top of the shelter just as you guys were getting out and those who survived were left in a daze for a while, useless for almost anything. We knew that the Brits were nearby and assumed that they wouldn't kill you but would take you prisoner, as all this was taking place well behind their front-line. It had already happened, and we were not wrong.'

'But you could have been wrong!' Orcande almost yelled, shaking his head in a fury and getting in haste to his feet. 'You could well have been wrong, and every one of these guys might have been killed because you couldn't spare your precious time to wait!'

He was clearly shocked. He knew *Wizard* well and believed him incapable of doing any damage on purpose. He was generous, open, and noble. He and his wife had even given him the moniker, *Tata*, to show the gratitude they felt towards him. He was godfather to his son, for Christ's sake! And now here it was that more than twenty years ago this man, whom he had learned to love so much, had abandoned a group of helpless soldiers in the middle of enemy territory, only to follow a plan!

'I can't understand how you can live with that!' he said. 'I don't know of anybody who could live with that!'

Outraged, he turned to go without looking back.

'No, Jorge you're wrong! You don't understand!' protested Damián Lucena as he moved towards his friend in an attempt to stop him. But *Wizard* grabbed his arm as he shook his head.

'Let him go!' he said. 'He'll soon find how to get over it!'

He sighed and turned his face to the embers.

'War is such a dreadful thing anyway!'

After a pause, he added: 'And we may never forget it,

but at least here we are, you and I, and we have been through it!'

Damián managed a sad smile and tapped his friend's shoulder.

'So it is, *Tata*! We are both here and we are both alive!'

Wizard felt the hand of his son reaching and lowered his gaze to look at the serious face, eyes widened either by the heat of the fire or because of what they had just witnessed. He drew the tiny body against his leg while he covered Damián's shoulders with his other arm.

When Annie came to see the roast she found them standing, her son between the men and all three staring silently at the embers.

The Toritos

For *Numa*, it was like returning to the old days. The three took turns behind the wheel but *Wizard* was still the one who lasted longer, as it was years ago when in the Navy.

They would be arriving in Bahia Blanca in less than an hour and they had arranged to meet *Bear* at La Paloma before Saturday. It was Wednesday, and he figured out they would board the ferry to Montevideo in approximately ten hours time. They were doing okay.

They arrived in Buenos Aires by the Southwestern Turnpike. It was ten thirty in the evening and the motorway was nearly empty, gleaming like hot metal under the orange glow of the streetlights. The ferry service would not begin until eight o'clock next morning and they were tired and badly in need of a shower. *Tony* suggested they try the Naval Station. 'We are still Navy, after all. Right? They might be cool and let us use an empty room,' he said.

They drove up Huergo Avenue and into the harbour area until they stopped in front of the iron gates of the Naval Station. Stepping out of the van they heard a sentry call, 'Stay right there!' and froze under the blinding beam of a searchlight.

'Come forward!' said the voice. *Wizard* advanced till he was close to the porthole from where the sentry was watching them. Still standing by the truck, *Tony* lit a cigarette.

As *Wizard* started back, *Tony* said 'We might be lucky, there used to be a group of divers stationed here.'

He was cut short by the noise of the gates opening. The OOD* appeared a few feet from the entrance, looking quite sullen.

'Seems like we blew it anyway!' said *Tony*, 'Get ready to sleep in the van!'

The officer signalled the trio to come forward and raised his hand to stop them as they crossed the gates.

'Stay there!' he said. 'How is it that you claim to be ex-Navy? Don't you know that you are not supposed to call on a unit outside working hours without prior notice unless it's been arranged or you are under orders? It's almost midnight and you come in all hunky-dory as if it were the most normal thing in the world! Luckily my sentry has the good sense to let me know! Do you have any identification?'

'And you, Lieutenant,' said *Wizard* suddenly, 'have you finally find out how to assemble a fuse?'

Taken aback, the officer took a step forward.

'*Wizard*?' he asked. 'You son of...! What the devil are you doing here? Weren't you living in Santa Cruz, you?'

They hugged, laughing.

'Come on in, please come on in!' said the officer, now all smiles.

'And you guys?' he asked turning towards *Numa* and *Tony*. 'Are you divers too?'

Wizard made quick introductions and the sentry closed the gate as they walked towards the building.

'What an amazing coincidence!' laughed the Lieutenant, whose name was Ahumada. 'Here I was in this damned shift covering up for a classmate whose child has got the 'flu – and look who decides to drop in on us! Really unexpected! Terrific!'

* (Duty) Officer of the Day.

Once inside the complex they climbed the stairs to the wardroom where two other officers were finishing their dinner.

'Are you guys hungry?' asked the Lieutenant.

'Frankly, we are,' answered *Tony*. 'But we don't want to be a nuisance, we're going out to get something and then we can come back. The only things we wanted to ask for were a shower and a corner in which we could lay down and rest until tomorrow morning, when we will board the ferry to Montevideo.'

'Not on my watch,' exclaimed the Lieutenant to the Midshipman sitting at the table. 'Let's see, Bedetti, give us a hand here! Can we find something for these guys?'

'Yes sir, Lieutenant!' answered the youngster, getting to his feet. 'No problem whatsoever! I'll fix it right away with the kitchen!'

The other officer stood up too. He was wearing First Lieutenant's bars.

'Lieutenant Furtado, my pleasure!' he said, putting out his hand.

'My pleasure!' said *Tony*, shaking it. 'Antonio Balbo. I was a NCO[*] with the Divers.'

Lieutenant Furtado turned to *Numa*, who greeted him with a short, 'Ismael Sastre, I was also with the Divers.'

As *Wizard* shook Furtado's hand he said, 'I know your father, I think. He was a submariner, wasn't he?'

'Yes, he retired seven years ago, his last posting was in Mar del Plata, as the CO[†] of the Submarine Force.'

'Precisely,' confirmed the *Wizard*. 'I remember him well. He's all right, I hope? Greet him from *Wizard* next

[*] Non-Commissioned Officer.
[†] Commanding Officer.

time you see him.'

'I will, be sure I will!' said Furtado as he sat down to continue his meal.

'Come on, *Wizard*, people,' encouraged the OOD. 'Take a seat and we'll soon bring something for you to munch! So long, no see, isn't it *Wiz*?' he added, grabbing a pair of chairs. 'And what are you guys doing here, if I may ask?'

Before any of them could answer, the Midshipman came back, confirming that steaks were on the way and the introductions were repeated. As they finished, Ahumada said, 'But then you are Lieutenant Mendoza's *Toritos*!* Or rather Captain Mendoza's! All here, surely you guys are cooking something! It's only *Bear* who's missing! I bet something very special is afoot!'

He looked quizzically in *Wizard*'s direction.

'Come on, *Wizard*, tell me!' he said, smiling. 'You can't leave me out! Not your best student!'

Wizard laughed. Ahumada had actually been his student in Naval Diving School. It was there that his joke about the fuse came from, because young Ahumada's attempts to carry out the mandatory task of setting off a submerged explosive charge had almost cost him his life.

The novices' training was already quite advanced, but while all the other students had long ago succeeded in completing that task, all the charges prepared by Ensign Ahumada had failed to explode. *Wizard* had thus scheduled some time after normal working hours to see him through the chore and now they had been at it for a while. When the fourth consecutive charge refused to go off, Ensign Ahumada ran out of patience and, taking advantage of the fact that *Wizard* was busy with other

* Little bulls.

equipment in the boat, he dived to see what had happened. He didn't get too deep, the charge exploded while he was still head down and the next thing he knew he was floating on the oily water belly-up like a dead catfish.

Later he would say that it felt as if a dozen mules had kicked him in unison. His diving mask was in pieces and he had a sliver of glass embedded next to the right eye. Besides that, the blast had perforated both his eardrums. He was hastily taken to sickbay and that same evening *Wizard* told him that the school director was considering expelling him from the course for 'being such an asshole'. The programme was scheduled to end in four weeks and, in any case, he wouldn't be able to dive for quite a while, but the reasons the director was acting upon were different. In his words, 'Idiots like this one kill people, but it takes years to train good people.'

Wizard argued his case. Ahumada was a good student and he knew he could turn him into a good combat diver. He proposed to have him work harder in order to compensate for the hours lost and eventually succeeded in getting him through the course.

Even before the unit was sent to the Malvinas, Navy divers had taken to calling the group Ahumada was referring to as 'Mendoza's Toritos'. Under the leadership of Lieutenant Eduardo Mendoza, they had worked together through several campaigns and they shared many colourful adventures. Each of the group's members excelled as specialists when compared to other divers in the unit, and together they worked more efficiently than all operational groups.

At that time *Tony* was by far the best paratrooper in the Navy. He was a Jump Leader of remarkable control. Stories of his coolness went around, as when his chute snarled on the plane's rudder and he hung there for a while because the fast release of his webbing failed to operate, or the time his canopy suddenly deflated just before landing because *Weasel* Contreras, his own chute on a streamer, had fallen on top of it.

On another occasion he had jumped out with a sail he had packed only minutes earlier, blindfolded. He did that after placing a bet with some of the *aficionados* of a flying club, and when the story came to light the Navy acknowledged his bravery with thirty days of unit arrest for endangering state property.

Bear was renowned among the divers for his strength. One story about him was that he once helped replace a flat tyre on a pick-up truck by getting under it and pushing it up on his back, because the jack was stuck and wouldn't work. He was aware of his strength, carried a massive bulk and had an impressive presence. But he was as passive as a hedgehog and it was almost impossible to get him angry.

Numa was a different matter altogether. The *Agrupación** had accepted him as a member in 1976 but he came from the outside. He was the son of a deceased Naval pilot.

It all started for him when he was staying at a summer house with his parents, enjoying the holidays after graduating from Naval High School. One morning his father drove up to a nearby bank to pay a bill. It was his misfortune that that very same day an ERP command decided to raid that bank. During the robbery, one of the masked attackers stopped in front of *Numa*'s dad and said, 'Hello there! Soon we're gonna bust you along with all your motherfucking friends.' Then he fired point-

---

* Combat Divers, *Agrupación de Buzos Tácticos*.

blank and shattered the man's knee.

The gunshot made its way down the tibia and finally lodged in the lower part close to the ankle, so the whole bone burst and had to be replaced. It took several operations and long therapy, but he worked like a horse, and a little more than a year after the mishap the Navy Medical Board agreed to let him fly again. He flew a couple of training missions in which everything seemed to go well, but later it was rumoured that you could tell he wasn't the same as before.

He killed himself during his third bomb target practice, but those who knew him always thought that something inside him had given way since the incident at the bank. The pilots who were flying with him when he fell, told that his plane left the formation suddenly and without any apparent reason and that he seemingly turned off his radio. Unable to stop him, they saw the aircraft enter a spin and then plunge out of control as if the pilot had shut down the engine.

The rescue team found the charred remains of the plane in the crab-infested banks between the sea and the Naval Air Station. They had to dig almost seven feet in the mud to get to the dead pilot.

The accident – which everybody thought had been a suicide – affected *Numa* deeply, and soon after he decided to leave the family house where everything reminded him of his father. He felt he needed time to think about his future and so he chose to go backpacking in Golfo Nuevo, where he and his dad had shared many good summers camping out.

He knew a girl in Puerto Madryn, and that also encouraged him. They had met during a visit that *Numa*'s school had made. He couldn't find her on arrival and later learned that she had married and moved to

Buenos Aires. Nevertheless, or perhaps because of that, he decided to stay, and it was there that he first learned to dive with the help of local divers.

He took heartily to this new activity and soon began to take tourists out on an outboard he rented from a retired fisherman. When he wasn't working he would run along the beach or practise boxing at the gym, but he also spent a great deal of time inspecting the shoals and exploring the Gulf. He lived alone and so didn't care to do much else, but each time the *Agrupación* showed up to train in the clear waters of the bay he would visit them in their bivouac and take a few divers along in their free time to dive for fish in the best shoals.

One year the unit arrived in March and the divers lodged inside the hangar on the Naval Air Station. The CO was an old friend of his father and *Numa* called on them after sunset, when he knew they would be getting ready to call it a day. He found him talking to two other officers and some NCOs, as they reviewed the communications protocols for the upcoming exercise.

'How are you doing, *Numa*?' said the CO when he saw him come in. 'Let me finish a few details here and I'll be with you!'

Numa sat on a stack of ammo boxes and struck up a conversation with some of the divers he knew from previous encounters. But as soon as the CO was done with his meeting he bade them goodnight and the two walked out together from the hangar.

'I called at your mother's the other day in Bahía Blanca,' began the CO as they ambled towards the officers' quarters. 'She's getting better everyday, I think. The loss of your old man hit her hard and these last months have surely been very difficult. Do you consider going back?'

'Just to visit her, but I couldn't live there. I'd rather live where I can go diving. It could be here, in Comodoro, Mar del Plata or Ushuaia, but it has to be by the sea. In Bahía Blanca the sea is a sorry joke.'

'Look here,' said the CO, stopping outside the Officer's Mess. 'You're already quite grown-up. Had you been younger I might have suggested that you apply to the Naval Academy, but it's too late for that now. However, you did go through Naval High School, and therefore you already have a military rank, albeit in the Reserves. Besides, you're good under water. I've talked about you with some of my divers and they actually think you're very good and cool under pressure. I could well use another officer and the Navy employs reservists in exchange for a salary that is really kind of symbolic, but on the other hand most of your expenses will be covered. If you're interested, it could be an interesting way to get over the winter, for I guess that once the temperature drops your business with tourists sort of dies out, right?'

'Funny that you should bring it up, sir. I've thought about it too. I've been considering going to Angra for a while now. I have friends there, former classmates. Some time ago they set up a diving school and they seem to be having a great time since.'

'I've no problem understanding that. It sounds like a tempting choice,' said the CO. 'Angra is a paradise for divers. In any case, give it a thought. I'm mentioning this because I believe that could also be a way to keep your ties with the Navy, which I have the impression may mean something to you.

'You know that your old man was much loved and highly respected among us,' he added, 'he left many good friends. These are not the best times for our country, there is a war going on and we need all the help we can get in order to win it. I understand that you might not consider it your war, but I can guarantee it was his.

'I also talked about this to your mother when I saw her last. You can imagine that fighting the guerrillas is everyday news in Bahía, much more talked about than here. She knows that what the Navy can offer has its risks, but the life that you live here makes her quite anxious anyway. So think about it and let me know once you've made up your mind. We are going to stay here for about ten days and if you're interested in taking this offer up there is some paperwork we have to go through and which may take a while.'

The divers returned to their base in Mar del Plata and in May *Numa* joined the unit as Midshipman(R) Ismael Sastre. To begin with he was appointed to run the Admin Office, but after two months dealing with spreadsheets and reports he asked to speak with the CO and told him that if that was all the Navy had to offer he was ready to resign the next day. Somehow amused by his cheek, but positively impressed with his impatience, the CO arranged for him to join the operational teams under supervision until he had found what suited him best and gradually carve out his reputation amongst the divers.

After some pestering, the XO* finally let him try his hand at one of the unit's miniature submarines, which carry two divers and a hefty bomb. These underwater delivery vehicles resemble more a torpedo than a submarine. In spite of a sliding cockpit-cover which is seldom used, the divers are constantly exposed to the water and breathe using regulators, so that riding them is like diving proper. They are heavy things, handling them effectively requires skill and much training.

* Executive Officer.

Sargeant Quispe, known to everyone as *Wizard*, was one of the best-trained pilots in the unit. He spent a whole morning helping *Numa* to get to know how to work the controls and that same afternoon took him out for a test dive.

With the submarine still above the surface, they unhooked the slings that held it fast to the crane's hook and took their places inside the cockpit. At *Wizard*'s sign, *Numa* took the painter in, made it fast to the side and pressed carefully on the throttle lever. They motored with their heads out of the water until they reached the tip of the seawall. *Numa* held the craft at an even depth using the diving rudders and, when they were some fifty metres from the wharf, he heard *Wizard* tell him, 'Now, sir, take her down carefully!'

He pushed the wheel forward and the mini-sub sank her bow, going for the bottom. He immediately felt the water flow pressing his mask against his face and got his head closer to the control panel, a little alarmed. Everything was happening too fast and for a moment he forgot to check the gauge he had before his very eyes. However, the growing pressure in his ears told him that they were sinking too fast, and then *Wizard* touched his shoulder.

From the corner of his eye he saw a hand signalling him to get the sub to level and decrease the speed. He eased the throttle lever and slowly pulled the control wheel backwards until he gradually managed to regain control and keep the sub at a constant depth.

As they had agreed, he made an underwater approach to the dredger that was moored alongside the pier, steering the sub by the compass that glowed on the instrument panel. After briefly breaking surface to aim at his target, he dived carefully and this time managed to stop the inertia that would have sent the sub even deeper. He then approached, cruising slowly, two metres under the surface.

Soon the green void ahead got darker, telling him that they were next to the dredger's hull. He stopped the propeller and let water into the immersion tanks, taking care to let the least possible air out so that the bubbles wouldn't be too visible from the surface. The mini-sub began to sink slowly. When she reached hull-fin depth he opened the compressed air valve and expelled the excess water to neutralize buoyancy at that depth.

The sub sank for a metre further and then she stopped. Only then *Wizard* left his seat in the cockpit and swam a couple of metres away from the sub. From there he checked the vehicle's position and gave *Numa* the success sign, showing both thumbs up. Then he returned to his place and signalled *Numa* to get some distance from the dredger and take the sub back to the surface.

As they motored back to their starting point *Wizard* congratulated him. 'That was sweet, sir! Let's do it again!' They did it another six times. In the end they were almost rigid with cold and only three divers had cared to wait for them to man the crane and take the sub back to her shelter. After they had secured the slings back in place they swam up to one of the pier ladders and were watching the divers hoist the sub when the XO arrived, driving a pick-up truck. He had seen the attacks from the pier and thought that the two last had been almost perfect.

'Almost perfect doesn't quite describe it, sir!' said *Wizard*, pointing an arm towards *Numa*. 'The chief here's a natural.'

From that day, *Wizard* and *Numa* became the

owners of the mini-submarines and took advantage of every possible chance to train on them.

A few months later, *Numa* enrolled in a skydiving course offered by a nearby flying club and bought a second-hand parachute. *Tony* Balbo introduced him to his friends in the competition environment and in no time he was hooked. Even though less than two years had passed since he had joined the unit, soon he had more jumps all told than the most experienced divers except his mentor, whose record was virtually unbeatable.

Time passed and new COs arrived. The rest of the officers also moved along and soon his permanence in the teams turned *Numa* into a key resource for the unit's efficiency. One good day Lieutenant Mendoza arrived, a blonde, baby-faced officer who swam like a shark. He was slightly taller than *Numa* and had finished his diver training the previous year. Somehow he failed to impress right away so nobody paid him a lot of attention, thinking that he might need some time to find his bearings before showing what he had.

That same winter the *Clarisa Montemayo* sank off Punta Mogotes, at a time when the fishing community of Mar del Plata was losing an average of two boats per year. The temerity of the skippers, inadequate or timeworn equipment, unreliable weather reports, all the conceivable factors converged to create a situation that, on average, left four or five families marked by loss every year. *Numa* knew only too well what it was like to be left behind.

The *Clarisa Montemayo* had sunk on a sandbar that almost never shows above the surface, but which is occasionally topped with surf at low tide. Colliding currents converge over it and *cazón* – the local variety of shark – is commonly found. There had been appalling weather lately and the Coast Guard launched a search for survivors just four hours after the boat was due in the harbour. But precisely on the same date, almost all the Coast Guard's resources had been summoned to Santa Fé province to assist in the evacuation of the victims of a sudden overflowing of the Paraná river.

In those years the Rescue Diving Service of the Mar del Plata Naval Base was an administrative division of the Diving School and lacked a permanent officer in charge. A team was rapidly put together and A.R.A. *Irigoyen* was readied to sail and inspect the wreck. On board was the school's portable decompression chamber.

Due to a whim of destiny none of the officers in the school who could have led the diving party was in Mar del Plata that week. The Director had no choice but to ask the Agrupación de Buzos Tácticos for an officer to take charge of the underwater search that was now considered indispensable, since two days of helicopter exploration hadn't yielded any traces of possible survivors. Lieutenant Mendoza got the job.

Knowing that *Numa* had dived many shipwrecks, the CO included him in the team along with *Wizard*, who was the unit's diving supervisor. A.R.A. *Irigoyen* sailed next morning at precisely six o'clock, towing a lateral-search sonar designed for shallow-water detection. Shortly before ten it picked up an echo that looked very much like a wreck. The CO decided to drop the anchor on the spot. They were just over two miles from the coast and three inflatable rubber boats were lowered to assist with the search.

Lieutenant Mendoza had planned to work with nine divers altogether. As the maximum depth was going to be twenty-five metres he designed a programme of 40-minute dives with two minutes' decompression stops that started at eighteen metres. It was a prudent scheme, for there was much swell.

He chose *Plunger* Pereyra as his buddy, an experienced diver who had been his instructor and whom he was used to dive with. *Wizard* would buddy up with *Bear* Contreras, a young, huge Petty Officer and combat diver whom *Numa* had also learned to trust. *Gringo* Nielsen – who was at the time one of the Diving School's instructors – would dive with *Mole* Nevares. Both were very good friends and worked well together. *Gringo* had the looks of a movie actor and was married to *Mole*'s sister, who had returned the favour by marrying *Gringo*'s in turn.

Numa paired up with *Tony* Balbo, his skydiving mentor. The ninth member of the party was *Don't-whine* Di Dorio. His task was to take care of the boats and the divers when the latter were on the surface and be ready to meet any need, in addition to soothing the anxiety of the ship's CO, who would most certainly require constant updating on the search.

The first pair down was the Lieutenant's. After them followed *Bear* and *Wizard*. The rest waited in the boats, sitting with their bottles donned, ready to dive at a call. As the minutes passed they got warmer inside their black neoprene suits and *Numa* jumped into the water to cool off. Just then, the Lieutenant and *Plunger* surfaced, carrying the body of one of the drowned fishermen.

An hour later they had recovered the bodies of five fishermen and that was all they finally got, for in further inspections they were unable to locate any others. Finally the CO decided to call the search off. They were getting ready to return to the ship when the CO called once more through the hand-held megaphone saying that they should try to recover the wreck's log too, for it could throw light on the reasons for the sinking.

As the rest managed to pile up the recovered bodies in the boats, the Lieutenant and Pereyra dived again. Handling the bodies was a difficult task, and looking at the diver's efforts made some of the ship's sailors sick.

Don't-whine was ready to send back a boat with bodies when *Tony* grabbed one of the bottles and, donning his swimming fins, said, 'Chief, send a diver after me, they are taking too long down there!' Then he dived.

'Holy fuck!' said Di Dorio and turned to *Wizard*, who was still wearing his bottles and weight belt but had taken off his fins. '*Wiz!*' he asked. 'Please, go! This idiot is doing a repeat dive, and I think he's already outside the table limits!'

Wizard didn't need to be told twice and jumped into the water, still holding his fins in one hand. Di Dorio put on the bottle he had taken off in order to work with the corpses. Looking at *Numa*, he said '*Tony* is right, sir. They've been too long down there! D'you mind if I go too and see what's up? I'm the only fresh diver that's left.'

'Go!' said *Numa*. 'I can manage well with these tigers here. But bring *Tony* back by the balls and let me know if something has happened.'

The corpses of the fishermen were slippery and moving them around was like hauling wet mattresses. They were filled with water and each weighed a ton. One had fallen from the boat and *Gringo* and *Mole* had just retrieved it when the rest of the divers emerged almost at the same time, hastily removing their bottles and with an urgency to get out of the water.

They climbed over the sides in a somewhat disorderly

fashion, pulling themselves up in a co-ordinated way so as not to tip the boats. The first one in was *Plunger* and almost immediately *Tony* climbed up on the other side. Then it was *Don't-whine*'s and *Wizard*'s turn while Lieutenant Mendoza climbed onto his boat from the bows, aided by *Bear*.

All seemed very excited as they removed their masks and spoke at the same time, laughing out loud, but *Numa* was perplexed and couldn't for his soul understand the reason for all this gaiety, because the entire task of retrieving the bodies had been truly unpleasant.

Eventually he was able to make sense of the conversation and found out what he had missed: once the first pair inspected the bridge without finding the log, *Plunger* dived further into the wreck and down to the wardroom situated one deck under the bridge. The compartment was quite dark, the only source of light being the hatchway that was partially obstructed by Lieutenant Mendoza as he dived head-first down the ladder. Nevertheless *Plunger* spotted a big notebook under a table and thought it probably was the logbook.

As he stretched his arm out to grab the book, the wreck shifted and came to rest on its starboard side. This change of position made a loose cargo spar on deck spin, sending the heavy chain that normally secured it to the side onto the bridge's closed portside door, locking its handles and rendering the mechanism impossible to operate from inside. As the starboard door was barred with the tangled remains of a heavy lifeboat, the divers were now effectively trapped inside.

They had not yet realised the new situation when Lieutenant Mendoza spotted a shark measuring around one and a half metres making a beeline for *Plunger* from a darkened corner. As the fish caught one of *Plunger*'s fins in its jaws pulling him from under the table, Mendoza got closer, trying to grab the head that shook violently from side to side, trying to get a better hold of *Plunger*'s leg.

Here came the funny part of the story, for lacking a better solution the Lieutenant punched and hit the animal on its snout. Although cushioned by the water, the blow was strong enough to startle the shark and make it open its jaws, thereby releasing its prey. Leaving the beast to find its bearings the divers swam up the ladder into the bridge, where they saw *Tony*'s masked face peeking through one of the portholes and finally became aware of the change in heeling.

As *Tony* tried to remove the chain to unlock the portside door handles, *Wizard* appeared at his side. They worked at it between them, but it was still too heavy. Within a few minutes *Don't-whine* showed up and, as the scene began resembling an underwater pow-wow, the shark resumed its attack inside the bridge.

According to *Plunger*, what followed was pretty much like a boxing training match. Probably thinking that the tactic he had used in the wardroom was effective, Mendoza hit the fish on its nose not once but three times with his fist, at which the shark decided to call it a day and swam out of the door as soon as it was opened. The presence of an angry shark in the water was what hastened the divers climbing into the boats.

This was the first job in which the group worked together. Their performance was so praised by the ship's CO that it became natural from then on to address them as an informal team inside the unit. The rest of the divers christened them *Los Toritos*, and word of their exploits – both real and imagined – would soon spread even beyond the Agrupación.

That same year the group was detached from San Antonio, Misiones, in a reconnaissance mission. They were supposed to locate and identify the principal trails used by smugglers which connected major roads with unlicenced airstrips built deep in the jungle. Small planes flew drugs in from Paraguay to the roughly built runways from which they were usually apportioned and stacked in hideaways for later retrieval.

Before they had been half a day in the mission it started raining and after seven days of continuous downpour the jungle turned into a swamp and all tracks became unrecognizable. They lost radio contact only ten hours after leaving and, by then, they had already crossed two river arms that had overflowed straight away. Aiming to escape the flood, Mendoza led the patrol to the foot of Sierra de La Victoria, where they made a bivouac and regained energies by eating the flesh of a *yacaré** and three monkeys that *Wizard* turned – according to *Tony* – into delicious dishes. When they finally made contact again twelve days later, National Guard helicopters had long been readied to take off as soon as the rain abated in order to start searching for them.

The group established its stand-alone identity after a series of undercover counter-terrorist operations in Mar del Plata and, in 1978, they were employed for nearly two months in a special reconnaissance assignment over the border with Chile, collecting military and hydrographic information in case war was declared.

While almost the whole unit was operating in Tierra del Fuego at that time, *los Toritos* were assigned special

* A type of caiman.

missions that the CO was coordinating with Army units operating in the area. In the course of an extended patrol, Mendoza decided it was worth trying to get to Puerto Natales in Chile, where a close inspection of the port facilities would result in acquisition of valuable intelligence for a possible attack.

Everyone in the group could acceptably mimic the way Chileans talk, it being a common gag throughout the Services. And so one night they crossed the border near the old *Laurita-Casas Viejas* pass, dressed as civilians. There they hailed a truck that took them to Natales, where they identified several places where defences were being set up, as well as other locations where they noticed uncommon military presence. They stopped at *La Caracola*, a bar in Baquedano Street, and lingered a while listening to the locals discuss the situation that everybody deemed was quite uncertain. It was there that a drunk got a bit overbearing and *Bear* had no better idea than to knock the lights out of him. The divers dragged him to a corner table where he wouldn't attract anybody's attention for a while and left without further fuss.

The little escapade almost finished Mendoza's career, but they did obtain valuable information, because the Chileans had garrisoned almost three regiments in town. They had used schools, sheds, two churches, a gym and even the fishing boats moored on the jetty to accommodate troops, in addition to scattering artillery pieces aimed towards the border throughout the area and camouflaging them under nets.

The problem was that *Numa* – who was admittedly a civilian – had taken part in the operation. Mendoza had arguments in his favour and an important one was that *Numa* had already taken part in counter-terrorism operations in Mar del Plata. These operations were – if one was to stick to the book – exclusively restricted to active-duty officers and enlisted personnel. The Navy was at fault and they knew it. But those were times for pragmatism and, in the absence of major accidents or casualties, they chose to drop the issue in the end.

Regardless of this, *Numa* had already fulfilled his contract as a Midshipman and was duly promoted. Three days after returning from Chile, he was called to the CO's office to receive his new bars and that evening the wardroom dined on his bill.

He was already an Ensign in the Naval Reserve. It was something to be proud of, but he still longed to see other things in addition to the Navy. So he decided to terminate his contract and travel to Brazil, where his friends in Angra dos Reis greeted his arrival with open arms.

An unexpected war would see him joining *los Toritos* once again.

Destiny Calls

'Overall, it's not a bad idea,' said Eduardo, looking at the buoys that resembled the coloured lights on a Christmas tree.

Bear thought briefly that the man showed his years. He hardly resembled the Lieutenant Mendoza he remembered, skinny and elastic.

'We certainly lose nothing by trying,' he said in an effort to sound positive while encouraging his friend to offer a more conclusive answer.

Eduardo nodded and took another drink of his gin and tonic.

'It's not bad and it's very interesting,' he added with a smile that erased years from his face.

'Our lion-coloured river,'* thought *Bear*, following his friend's eyes as they scanned the choppy brown waters beyond the windowpane. They were in one of Buenos Aires' waterfront restaurants. Contrasting with the dull shades of the river, everything inside the place looked too shiny. He remembered with nostalgia the rickety *carritos* where he had so many times enjoyed a *choripán*† without reflecting for a moment on the quality of the service. He was not happy with the change. Though the *carritos* had looked – and probably were – filthy, they were authentic. They had soul. These new

* Popular reference to the La Plata River. It was coined by the Argentine national poet, Leopoldo Lugones (1874 – 1938).
† Pork sausage sandwich, a typical starter on *asados* (barbecues).

restaurants that replaced them were just shiny covers for the emptiness and greed of their owners.

Perhaps he too was getting old, but he really missed things like being able to call the waiter by his name or say hello to the owner with the self-confidence of a long-time customer. But now one couldn't even spot the owners, they wouldn't even show up to see how business was going.

Eduardo had told him that he lived in Mar del Plata and worked in a shipyard. It was good business: they were selling much to Brazil. 'I left the Navy when I felt there was nothing else left for me there,' he said, suddenly changing the subject. 'Once you reach a certain rank there's almost no adventure left, it's another kind of action. You spend the day discussing formalities, procedures or precedence matters, putting together budget proposals for which there are never enough funds. I was bored and it showed. But what about you?' he asked, 'how come you ended up in Uruguay?'

'You know, sir, it was purely by chance!' he answered. 'I left the Navy before you, as you may have heard.'

'Yes, I did,' confirmed Eduardo, 'and I was really surprised, for the last time we saw each other it seemed to me that you were quite satisfied with your lot.'

'Well, what happened to me is pretty much like what happened to you. I was bored too. Once I finished my contract and not knowing better then, I looked for a job on the waterfront. I found it in the tugboats, where they were more than ready to hire an able hand. I had some friends there, but the whole thing was very uncertain to think about it as steady. Five or six months after that, a great-aunt of mine appeared out of the blue. I had not seen her or heard from her since I was a kid, but she was really nice and apparently had loved my mother very much. She had inherited some land in Uruguay from her late husband. She was dying, had no children and didn't want it to fall into the hands of the Government.

'She knew I had enlisted and managed to locate me through the Bureau of Personnel, who gave her my number. When she called, I had had enough of the tugboats and was working shifts as a driver for a car rental in Avellaneda. I hardly remembered her, but was curious and dropped off by her place in Adrogué. It was a huge house with lots of lemon trees in the garden. I got used to visiting. She had led quite an interesting life and it was entertaining to listen to her telling about it. She was actually my father's aunt. He died when I was thirteen. It was then that I decided to enlist in the Navy. I was desperate to leave and couldn't think of anything else. I'm not boring you, am I?'

'Certainly not!' said Eduardo as he lifted his arm to get the waiter's attention. 'Please continue, I'm re-discovering you!'

'Ok. During one of those visits she told me about this property. She had never been to it, didn't even know it very well, where it lay, or how big it was. I was the only relative she knew who was still alive and she wanted me to look into its legal state and visit it if possible. I was quite busy at the time trying to find an occupation that could last, but I had grown very fond of her and told her I would see about it. Of course I never meant to take the commitment seriously, God knows that the least I needed was to go to Uruguay to inspect a wasteland! But there you have it. The truth is that nobody knows who they work for.'

The waiter approached and Eduardo asked for a couple of beers and small snacks.

'Next thing I knew,' continued *Bear*, 'some two weeks

after one of my calls I received a letter from a lawyer's office. At first I thought that there had been some kind of mistake, for I have always tried to keep those birds at a distance. Nevertheless I phoned them and they confirmed that there was no mistake. They wanted to talk to me in connection with the will of Doña Marta Acuña, my great-aunt. So I found out that she had died six days before I got the letter.'

Here *Bear* fell silent for a while and Eduardo, already guessing what his friend's story would come to, couldn't but reflect once more on how quirky life can be.

'One of her neighbours had asked for a cup of tea and saw her from the street and through the window, sitting very quiet on her rocking chair with a half-knitted scarf on her lap. She thought she had fallen asleep but realised something was on when my great-aunt didn't get up to answer the doorbell. She might have seen it coming, for she had made her will the day before and put it together with other outgoing mail on top of her desk, sealed and addressed to her lawyers. She named me as the universal heir and I inherited everything she had owned, including the house with the lemon trees. But what really changed my life was that the little piece of land in Uruguay that turned out to be a property of 3,700 hectares in La Paloma and which included almost seven miles of coastline. And so it all began. I sold the house, resigned from my job and crossed the river to check my property.'

The waiter returned with the order and placed it on the table.

'I didn't know shit then about farming, so I started by calling on the neighbours next door to hear whether somebody could update me on the value and prospects of the property and hopefully help me settle in. A Basque named Zorraguieta offered to lodge me until I had finished making the house functional. He also advised me to buy cattle, took me along to farm markets where he was known and helped me design the pens and wire the paddocks. Once I was settled in, he helped me begin dairy production and together we planted some crops. Now it's all on its way. A very nice man, he really taught me everything, the Basque. But that's only part of the story,' he said, raising his mug in a toast.

'Here's to you, sir! To this encounter!' Eduardo raised his mug and they drank.

'So far it sounds like an incredible story!' said Eduardo, encouraging his friend to continue. 'What happened next?'

'Well,' continued *Bear*, 'the Basque began to introduce me to his friends. One of them owns a property bordering mine and in the beginning didn't want to have anything to do with me, but as soon as he realised that I had come to stay he changed his mind. We finally got together and became very good friends. Here comes the interesting part, because he is a Brit who also took part in the war. What's more, he is the Sergeant who found the zombies we left behind when we were on our way to the front. You remember them, I'm sure?'

Eduardo's eyes narrowed.

'This can't be true!' he said.

'Well, it is!' insisted *Bear*, satisfied with the effect of his story. 'Just as I'm telling you! He was a patrol commander, and he remembers everything. You can just imagine, sir, all the things we talked about.'

Eduardo nodded. 'Incredible,' he said and got suddenly to his feet. 'It's really a fascinating story, *Bear*, but you will have to excuse me for a second. I have really been wanting to take a leak since we came here and if I don't do it now I think I'll explode.'

Watching Eduardo negotiate his way among the tables, *Bear* tried to remember the last time he had seen him and concluded that it had probably happened some four years after the war.

That war had caused most of the people he knew to change radically. While many lost their dash and were humbled into almost insignificance, others woke to a newfound self-assurance that bordered on provocation, as if they had discovered a strength they didn't know they had. Seeing Eduardo once again made him reflect on the persistence of the bond they shared and he thought −not for the first time − that to him, war had been good.

It didn't make it less tragic, though. He knew he had been especially lucky and there had been instances in which he was sure he was going to die. But the balance was still positive and he could not help feeling something approaching nostalgia every time he remembered those months.

As he scanned the restaurant distractedly he saw a familiar face in a nearby group. He remembered her well: he had seen her at a memorial service in Mar del Plata, shortly after the war. She had been once engaged to a marine officer who served in the Comandos Anfibios* and there he had a clear example of how war fucked up lives, for the husband-to-be never returned from the Islands.

He knew the guy. He had been killed at Darwin. They met in the Islands, though *Bear* had heard about him many times. The guy was almost a legend. It was

* Agrupación de Comandos Anfibios (Amphibious
Commandos) is the Special Forces unit of the Argentine
Marines.

rumoured that he had handled very dangerous jobs in the Dirty War. They ran into each other near Fitzroy, when *Bear* was making his way back to the bivouac after inspecting a landscape feature that, from a distance, looked like a beached craft. Lieutenant Mendoza had spotted it a day before and wondered whether it might still be seaworthy. He wanted to have a closer look, but things became complicated with the laying of some antennas and, as dusk was setting, he chose to send him alone for a quick glance.

He was on the way back from checking what turned out to be a large stone, when the man emerged from behind a boulder, aiming a rifle at him.

'What the fuck are you doing here?' he asked.

Bear froze on the spot. The apparition wore cammies without any insignia and had a shoulder strap hung with hand grenades around the neck. 'A war lunatic,' he thought.

'Mind your rifle,' he said. 'I'm a naval NCO.'

The rifle's muzzle didn't move.

'I asked what the fuck are you doing here,' repeated the stranger. *Bear* said he was returning to his position, and the man asked who was his Section Commander.

'First Lieutenant Mendoza,' said *Bear*, regretting his big mouth on the spot, for it dawned on him he had no idea whom he was addressing.

'*Baby Face* Mendoza?' asked the man with a derisive laugh. 'And some idiots say life lacks a sense of humour!' He lowered the rifle's muzzle and cut to a dry laughter in what *Bear* thought was a pretty neat piece of acting. Then he launched on a very martial speech, ordering him to convey to Eduardo that though the Brits had not yet arrived (they were actually landing as he spoke, but few Argentines knew it yet) to order someone to carry out a reconnaissance on his own was an act of imbecility. With this he turned his back on him and added a brisk 'Follow me!'

Bear followed.

When they entered the cave he saw a group of seated ranks, their backs against the wall. The place was tight and well-concealed. It was very dark and he could not distinguish the faces well, but he saw his escort speaking to a dark-haired man with whiskers. He recognised the man. He was a marine NCO he had seen in the ESIM.*

The NCO looked at him and asked if he was lost. *Bear* explained his situation once more, adding that he should leave because he was expected back. Suddenly he was aware that except for him everybody was very silent. There was a tension in these marines that contrasted sharply with the merry attitude of the divers. It was absurd, but their coolness made him feel they were testing him. The guy with the grenades sat down and said it was too late to venture outside alone. It was safer to spend the night and return to his group with the first light. In any case, he added, they had probably started digging already their night positions.

Realising that they didn't intend to let him leave before dawn, *Bear* insisted that he had orders to follow.

The grenade guy gave him a funny look and said that if Lieutenant Mendoza had sent him alone it was surely because he trusted that he could take sound decisions, among them to wait for light to come back before returning. He added that if he were to go back now it was likely he would get lost if a trigger-happy sentry didn't kill him before. Whoever that guy was, *Bear* realised that he was right. He dropped the issue, but was still piqued

---

* The Marine's NCO school in Mar del Plata.

by the imperative tone the guy used.

'Excuse me,' he said. 'Whom am I speaking with?'

Removing the shoulder strap from his neck, the guy said: 'You are talking to Lovak, Lieutenant Agustín Lovak. Comandos Anfibios.'

Now Mendoza was making his way back through the tables.

'And how did you come to talk about all this, how is it that you became aware that he was talking about the same guys?' he asked, referring to the zombies' episode.

'To begin with, we realised pretty fast that we had been operating in the same area,' replied *Bear*. 'The zombies' story came up after a while, one afternoon when we were inspecting a defective windmill. I don't remember what we were talking about when Patrick – he's called Patrick, this Brit – told me I was the second Argentine he knew that had been in the same area as his section. I asked who the other one was, and he told me he was a former Army conscript whom they had taken prisoner along with some other recruits.

'Years after the war, a friend of Patrick's foreman's niece showed up at the farm looking for a job. He was one of these conscripts. Talk about a small world, sir!

'They recognised each other immediately. They stood speechless until the guy said he wouldn't ask for anything, for Patrick had once given him more than anybody could imagine. The *gringo* is still moved when he tells the story. The man works in the farm today and he is one of the conscripts we left behind that time. When I told Patrick our part of the story, he couldn't believe the coincidence.

'Together we figured that they must have found them not later than a couple of days after we did. By then they were already quite organised and had apparently chosen a leader, a naval volunteer named Aranda who was slightly older than the rest and seemed to have a clearer idea of the situation than any other among them. He had them bury the dead and gather whatever weapons and rations were remaining. His plans had been to march north until they hit the coast where they would turn eastward and try to get to Puerto Argentino or find some Argentine unit who could take them in. But they did not have a clue where the front was. In any case, they had just started off when Patrick ran into them.

'According to him they were six in total. If we count the Sergeant whose remains – as you may recall – we saw scattered around, there had originally been thirteen, although Salinas said they were fourteen. Salinas was the guy we took with us along with Ricardes, the little one on the stretcher.'

Eduardo nodded and tried to focus on what *Bear* was saying. He could not help thinking that they were remembering one of the most exciting moments of his life and speculated that those would probably be the facts for which someday somebody may remember him.

'Five had died in the explosion,' continued *Bear,* 'and a few hours later the rest were almost back to normal. According to Patrick this Aranda guy was quite observant and as soon as he saw the Brits he started shooting at them and shouting orders to the conscripts, forcing them to seek cover.

'But their fire lacked cohesion. It wasn't regular and they were unable to keep the cadence. Patrick soon realised they were facing a few untrained conscripts. He could manage a little Spanish and shouted that they were behind British lines, that the British were already entering Stanley and that there was no sense in getting killed.

'Aranda wouldn't yield, but the resistance he was putting up was weak. Still, Patrick couldn't see the point of risking his men. He waited until dark, surrounded Aranda's position and captured the conscripts without giving them any chance to react. Only Aranda and a guy called Zamudio tried to resist, but they didn't have their weapons ready and the Brits hit them with their rifle butts, bound them up and waited for dawn.

'Once Patrick realised the state of his captives he guessed there was not much to fear from them and explained once again what he had said about the progress of the war. He told them they were prisoners and that if they tried to escape his men would shoot to kill. Then he untied their wrists and all shared some biscuits before starting towards Puerto Argentino (Stanley).

'According to him, they marched for almost two days. During the first night Aranda tried to escape together with a José Reche and everything went pretty well for them until Reche stumbled over a sharp stone. He could not walk, had a nasty cut over the knee and asked Aranda to leave him there and keep moving on. Aranda helped him to a group of rocks where he was able to support his back, and there he sat as still as possible. It was still very dark for him to see, but soon he heard a voice in broken Spanish telling him not to move or else he would be shot.

'Then as soon as there was light enough he saw Patrick lying on the floor just metres from him, propped on his elbows and aiming his rifle at him. Patrick got up, came forward and offered his shoulder as support. "C'mon!" he said. "We're going to freeze here." Today, Reche is married to the daughter of Patrick's foreman.'

'And what happened to the naval volunteer, to Aranda?' asked Eduardo. 'Did he ever make it back?'

'Aranda's story is quite crazy too. 'Funny enough, I also met him. It happened in Corrientes, at the airport. I was standing by a kiosk. It was another of these amazing coincidences. He works as a journalist in Goya, he writes about local politics.

'He was talking to a short man who must have been somehow deaf, for it was almost impossible not to hear what he was saying. He was talking about the Malvinas. My flight was delayed and I was bored, so I introduced myself and proposed we had a beer together. We talked for hours, there was a big storm that day and the planes seemed to avoid Corrientes as if the place had caught the plague. The man is a compulsive talker. At one point he told about how he had once landed with a section inside a cave and how almost half of them had been killed when a bomb landed in the entrance of their refuge. He then recounted how we had run into them and was quite surprised when I told him I had been on the party. In any case, he agreed that we had made the right decision. There was no way in which we would have been able to take them along. He had an incredible life. He had been a Monto in the '70s.'

'What you say is really amazing,' interrupted Eduardo. 'It seems incredible, so much of what you tell probably happened by chance, but nevertheless it is as if the Malvinas forged links that will follow us to our graves.'

They had not touched the food and *Bear* said, 'Let's eat something, sir. If not we might not be able to walk, for we have drunk a lot.'

Eduardo laughed.

'But you said that they were six,' he said. 'D'you know something about the rest? Did you ever meet any of them again?'

'I know of one who works with *Wizard*,' replied *Bear*, drawing a hairline with his fingernail on the tablecloth. 'Don't know nothing about the others but I never really made an effort to find them. I imagine they kept on with their lives and tried to put those memories behind. The truth is that each one owes a huge debt to Patrick, they could have killed them all.'

'Why would they do something like that?' asked Eduardo.

'You're right, come to think about it,' said *Bear*, suddenly remembering the cave with the commandos and their Lieutenant called Lovak. 'What for?'

Debit and Credit

The bar at the airport was chock-full. They had already finished their lunch and were enjoying a third beer. *Bear* had lost all notion of time and although he tried hard he couldn't remember having seen Aranda's face before.

Aranda, in contrast, had almost photographic memory. Now they were talking of what they had been doing before the war and how each one had ended up in the Malvinas.

'To me, it all began in an empty house in Tigre,' said Aranda, setting the half-emptied glass on the table. 'Central Command had summoned a meeting to organize a strike. We were to take over the Military Hospital while the 2nd column mounted a diversionary attack on the Police Main Garage. The plan was to destroy their logistic chain, for we knew they were using the hospital to store weapons.

'Of course you couldn't know in advance how the exact deployment was going to be. Information like that would be delivered on the spot or be simply bogus in order to confuse the police or the military, for there was always a chance that it could be leaked. A number of operations screwed up because of motherfuckers acting as moles and you never really knew who you were talking to.

'We had used the house before and so we went to the rendezvous without any reservations and even took some shortcuts regarding normal procedures, for it's clear that we could have been more alert. Anyway, we were climbing down the stairs to the basement when

Russian stopped on the tracks and whispered us to keep still.

'Justino froze as if he had seen a ghost. It was very dark and from the start the whole thing seemed a little fishy, so that when I heard a "click" I thought we were screwed. Justino's face was white like paper. Using his fingers, *Russian* traced a wire over Justino's leg, just below his front pocket.

'"Now don't even think of moving!" he said as he ducked under. Justino was hardly breathing. He stared at me like a rat that's been trapped. He was terrorised by the thought that whatever it was it would explode right then and bury us in the rubble.

'We listened as *Russian* fumbled in the basement and I remember I was impressed by the balls that the son of a bitch showed. At that stage I thought I knew him quite well, we had been together in some jobs. Small break-ins, courier gigs and things like that. They were short yet crucial jobs that could suddenly turn very complicated. The motherfucker worked well, he was no dodger and spoke little. He also had luck on his side and somehow managed to land always safely.

'It was *Marita* who brought him in, she told us he was studying to be an engineer and they had met during a yoga class. *Marita* didn't normally take bullshit from anybody but it was obvious that *Russian* was a sucker for her or at least he played the part. He was persistent and admittedly had looks. At first his insistence upset her. *Marita* wasn't what you'd call the romantic type. But she finally yielded and they ended up together. He rented a flat there where Junín makes a corner with Las Heras. They met there, they were sleeping together but *Marita* was never one to go all the way with guys.

'One day she brought him along. They were already

seeing each other almost every day and a few of us were curious, you know? We knew Marita's time was not spent in taking care of a sick mother. *Insect* was at that meeting too. He showed up randomly and always carried some top quality dope, so that in the end the thing turned into a kind of party and *Russian* joined in the smoking and acid-dropping without any manifest restraint.

'I think we recruited him there and then, but I was too high that night so I don't remember whether we went through all the usual formalities with him. After that night we saw him often and he gradually got in the game. One afternoon in Almagro I introduced him to two fellows from the Orga who had commissioned me to monitor a transfer. It was the first time he came along. I I think it all started there.

'But that evening Justino and I were waiting for him to return from the basement when we heard steps above us. I took out the piece I always carried under my belt. It was too dark to see Justino's face but I had already seen him so scared that I think he wouldn't have been able to do anything anyway. When I turned to climb I found the mouth end of a sawn-off shotgun looking at me.

'"Drop that and come up here!" said the copper as he climbed backwards, still aiming at me.

'*Russian* reappeared from below and took the gun from my hand, pushing aside Justino, who was still frozen stupid as he tried to digest the notion that the son of a bitch had sold us over.'

Rabbit Aranda paused. Other passengers whose planes had been delayed were trying to kill time snooping aimlessly through the few news-stands, while the majority of those fortunate enough to have a chair dozed or stared vacantly in front. *Bear* wondered how many of them may also have interesting stories from those times. But then Aranda returned to his.

'I never saw him again until the war. ESMA* gossip said that either he or a guy who looked a lot like him kept on working a long time from inside the Orga, betraying people and claiming to be one of us. Instead of an engineering student he was a naval officer.

'I always suspected that it was because of him that they finally got Marita. One night one of their squads arrived at her place. Those visits were very bad news. She had been expecting a friend and left her front door unlocked. They came in, beat her up for a long time and threw her out the window. The flat was on the seventh floor. Goodbye Marita! Or maybe she jumped herself, I don't know. In any case, her friend found the mess on the pavement. You remember in those times episodes like that were not uncommon.

'But I had no doubt that it was the *Russian* who tipped them. The girl was a pearl. She lived for the Orga. They trashed her place, took away all her books and arranged it to look like a break-in. They even made a neighbour appear as a witness so the case was filed as burglary followed by murder. When I learned about it I swore I'd kill him.

'Justino and I had a better fate. Justino was tortured in Campana, the Army used to run a prisoners' camp there. He was released in '81 and by then he was somebody else. They took everything out of him. They downright broke him, but they let him live. I saw him once in a grill in Cabildo, he was working there as a

* The Navy's NCO school. Part of the building complex where the school functioned up to the '80s was used under the military government as a detention centre for terrorists.

waiter. He saw me and started crying, the sissy. It pissed me, so much that I told him I had always thought he was a real cunt.

'Sad, he probably didn't deserve it! Sometimes it's easy to forget what life can do to you. For two years I had to take their crap in ESMA and you wouldn't like to hear the details. I don't know if you were ever there, you must have been quite young then. When I left it was to go to the hospital, because in addition to all the bones they had crushed, one of the doctors there thought I had a rare type of cancer and would make for an interesting study case before I kicked the bucket. *An interesting study case!*' he laughed. 'That's what I call being a true son of a bitch!

'In any case, they sent me to the Churruca* and there I met a radiologist who had also been in the Orga. He was older than me and had given up the fight. He said that he was very happy to have left all that behind. He was a bit of a philosopher, but at that time I could only see the coward in him. Anyway, he helped me to escape. One night he asked the sentry at my door to help him with bringing up a bed from the floor below, for the lifts had stopped working. As he wheeled me back from an X-ray session, he tipped me about his plan and gave me a copy of the key to my room. He also managed to hide some clothes and a little money under my bedclothes. When the soldier came back I had already left the building.

'He was a good man, in his own way. Once on the street, I discovered he had stuck a note in the pocket of

* Churruca Hospital, in Parque Patricios – almost in the centre of Buenos Aires – is the hospital assigned to the Federal Police.

the jacket I was wearing. My first impulse was to throw it away but I changed my mind, after all he had put himself at considerable risk to get me out. It showed as to how he had begun attending PC[*] meetings already as a boy, then rose up to be a big fish in the Party until something very wrong happened.

'It happened the day Perón chased the Orga out of the square.[†] He had always supported him and so his whole world collapsed, and in a meeting shortly after he exchanged words publicly with another big shot. Then one night as he returned from a reunion with UOM[‡] leaders, someone shot his wife and kids. He claimed he recognised the car where the shots came from and knew it was the Orga. Also, as the killers left they shouted 'You have paid for your treason!'

'He swore it was slander: he had never given any information away. He added that I was healthy, whoever had said that I had cancer had probably not seen a cancer in his frigging life. If I still wished to live he advised me to hang up my gloves and get me a normal life. I never knew his real name. He signed the note as Adrián.

'Two weeks later, we invaded the Malvinas. I had all this anger. I forgot about Justino, the *Russian*, the Orga and the doctors. I wanted something very strong, something that either could change my life completely or finish it for good. So I joined as a volunteer.'

Another pause of *Rabbit* shifted *Bear*'s attention to a

[*] Argentine Communist Party.
[†] On 1st May 1974, during one of the last speeches he held from the balcony of the Casa Rosada (the Presidential Palace overlooking Plaza de Mayo), Perón stripped Montoneros of their claimed allegiance to Perónism and chased them out of the Plaza, calling them stupid and infantile.
[‡] Union of Metallurgic Workers.

new delay of his flight, which was being announced through the loudspeakers. This was so Argentina, he thought, pitying the girl behind the airline's counter as she tried to placate a group of angry passengers. He reflected with sadness that the country was headed for the pit. There was nothing to do about it. So many dead, so many lives ruined, and the place was still the same nuthouse almost thirty years later.

'Contreras you said, was it?' asked Aranda. He didn't remember having seen him before. He remembered the explosion, yes, as they came out of the hole. He remembered that he and almost all who survived the blast were like idiots for a while, some took hours to see well again and many lost their hearing for most of the day. He remembered the uniforms, Lieutenant Mendoza and *Wizard*, but *Bear* he didn't.

Bear nodded. 'Long time ago...'

'I was quite all right when you guys found us,' continued Aranda. 'Pretty much so, but I felt weak. When it was clear that you were not planning to wait or take us along I thought the conscripts would probably die because they didn't have a clue, so I decided to stay. It wasn't that I felt bad about you leaving. You couldn't move fast with us in tow. I had come there to fight and it was the same if I met the Brits there or somewhere else. Besides, the conscripts were nice kids, so I played the zombie until you left.

'Two days later the Brits showed up. I tried to organize a resistance but we were just five and only three were able to understand what was happening. For them it must have been like fishing with a net, they surrounded us and we had to surrender. A Sergeant led them. He was a decent man. He warned us not to try anything or they would kill us and left us to walk without being bound.

'That night I tried to escape. With me came Reche, a conscript who was always quarreling with Gatica, who died at the explosion. He moved fast but stumbled and fell over a sharp stone and sort of broke his knee.

'It must have been very painful, but he never said a word. When I got to him he said "Keep on, you keep on!" It was pitch dark. You couldn't see shit. I told him I could carry him but he knew I was lying: I couldn't take him anywhere if I wanted to escape. I had nothing to leave with him so I helped him to a bunch of rocks. He grabbed my hand very hard, maybe because of the pain or to say goodbye. I kissed his head and said nothing but it felt like shit, leaving him there. I ran a long way. I wanted to put the English, Reche and the whole fucking world behind.

'When morning came I was completely lost. I was soaked too, but kept on walking. I had a fever and was nearly frozen. On the second night I heard people and hid behind a big stone, as still as I could. I was afraid that I was becoming delirious and again it was dark. You probably remember how black the nights can get down there. But from time to time the explosions lit up the horizon. One of the flashes showed a uniformed figure very close to where I was. It couldn't have lasted more than a couple of seconds, but it was enough for him to see me and then he cried in Spanish, 'Sir! There's a man here. Seems alive.'

'English or ours?'

'I think he's ours,' said the guy, and then both were towering above me. I was somehow relieved, at least these were Argentines. One of them pointed a red torch to my face and asked me if I could hear him.

'The torch blinked and then the same voice said, 'Wait a minute here! *Rabbit*?

'It was *Russian*.

'I couldn't believe the coincidence of finding the son of a bitch out there. I was convinced it was a sort of message. Finally the time had come to make him pay, the fucking bastard! I didn't know how I was going to do it but I think I even thanked God for the opportunity he offered me to get even. For the sake of *Marita*, Justino and all our people the weasel had helped to destroy. I fainted, I think from pure joy.

'When I came to we were inside what looked like a cave. It occurred to me that there were caves wherever I went. There were weapons everywhere. Assault rifles, ammo, MAG* crates I think, half opened. There also was a mug on top of a rickety alcohol burner. They had placed me in a corner, under a sleeping bag that stank of sheep fat. *Russian* was talking. He was telling how he had infiltrated the Orga. "I shared many screwy situations with that guy over there," he said, pointing to where I was.

'A marine who carried a black moustache and had military written all over his face turned to me and asked, "Are we back?"

'I didn't answer. I wanted to hear what *Russian* had to say. The more I heard, the angrier I got. I just wanted a chance, for I had made up my mind to kill him. As slowly as possible, too.

'I don't know how long we were in there. Maybe it wasn't more than two or three days but I saw *Russian* go out several times. They went in groups, him and perhaps two or three marines. They would be a while and almost invariably returned with stuff. Bits of personal

---

* French-made light machine gun normally fired using a tripod.

equipment, ammo, the odd weapon or fresh batteries. Once they even came back with combat rations. Everything seemed to come from the Brits, and I thought that they were either scavenging the dead or else they had found a depot and were depleting it.

'It all changed one afternoon when *Russian* arrived pretty strung and with blood all over his parka. They had tried to ambush a patrol – I realised then that that was their gig – but this time the Brits counter-ambushed them. He had managed to break but his two buddies had been killed. To me this reeked of his ways. There he was once again, not surprisingly letting others bear the brunt. But at least this time he hadn't gotten out intact, a bullet had gone clean through his left shoulder. His arm hung limp. Thinking that he might have been tailed, he wanted us to leave. As the marines gathered all they could take and smashed what was being left behind, he talked to me for the first time.

'"What do you wanna do?" he asked. "You may stay here. I doubt that the Brits will kill you, you don't carry a gun and are weak enough to pose a threat."

'I had serious doubts about the Brits' merciful tendencies and thought it better to get out and fight rather than getting killed like a dog. Neither did I think much of their gallantry, much less after an ambush. So I said I would go with them and he handed me an AUG*, a belt with two full magazines and a pouch of loose ammo. The rifle was surprisingly light compared to the FAL.

'He could do that kind of thing, *Russian*.'

Aranda shrugged and fell silent. Even though he had so far done nothing but listen, *Bear* still felt he should not disrupt the man's ruminations. He was somehow

---

* Austrian-made assault rifle.

moved by the story and could see that almost twenty years after the war Aranda was still disturbed by his burden.

As for him, he had chosen the future. He refused to stay anchored to a history that had not been part of his personal experience. Most of the 70s he had spent at sea in vessels of the Antarctic Command. Nothing memorable there, but he was aware that for most of his generation the past was painful territory: whether they saw themselves as guilty or innocent, dreamers or oppressors, actors or spectators, most of them had been saddened forever. There were few who could claim never having experienced strong bitterness or extreme frustration. To some these were just bad memories, but these people hurt.

Probably his new life across the river made him see things under a different light, he thought. Argentina seemed constantly bent on looking back.

His flight was voiced through the tannoy system and he stood up. Aranda's gaze was fixed on the table. He was still lost in his reveries.

'I'm leaving, friend Aranda!' he said, gesturing towards the ceiling. 'They have just called my flight.'

Aranda looked at him with a puzzled expression. Then he stood up and stretched his hand. He looked at him anew, as if returning from very far away.

'Cáceres, right?' *Bear* nodded a smile. 'It was nice. I hope I didn't bore you. I know I talk too much!'

'Don't worry,' answered *Bear*, shaking the stretched hand. 'One doesn't find fellow survivors every day. I will pass your greetings over to Reche and the Brit. Call on us one day, now that you know where we live. I wish you good luck. I hope that you won't need to wait too long for your plane.'

'Don't you worry about that,' said Aranda. 'If there's something I've learned it is patience.'

Before disappearing through the boarding gate, *Bear* turned to wave goodbye. It was no use. He saw *Rabbit* sitting at the table, his eyes staring at the empty glasses, probably once again lost in his memories.

Even

Despite the fact that he thought everything happens for a reason, *Rabbit* couldn't help feeling frustrated once he realised how hard it would be to carry out his revenge. It was his own attitude that bothered him the most, for before his encounter with *Russian* he had often imagined his vengeance in ghastly detail. Now, for some reason, during those few days with the bastard finally at hand, he seemed to have lost the drive to carry it out.

It was night and they had stopped to rest. He had a weapon which gave him the possibility of finishing *Russian*, who sat a little further off with his back against the rocks, separated from the rest of the group. He moved and sat beside the man he hated, his legs extended flat and their boots almost touching.

'I guess you still want to kill me?' asked *Russian* without opening his eyes.

'You know you're a son of a bitch and I've come here to collect,' he answered. 'Do you really want to die so much?'

'See this?' said *Russian*, sliding his thumb under the shoulder strap where the hand grenades hung like a garlic braid.

Rabbit did not answer. He couldn't see anything in the dark, but he could feel *Russian*'s gesture.

'I carry these like this in order to make sure I blow to hell if they get me. Of course I would like to carry along some of them, too. Anyway, when that happens, you're going to think that justice has been well served. To me, it's going to be a blessing.'

'It won't be justice if you die fighting,' said *Rabbit* looking straight ahead and into the dissolving darkness. 'Scumbags like you should die miserably and asking for forgiveness.'

He fell silent. He was too choked by anger to talk quietly with the man he knew had destroyed so many lives, wrecked so many efforts and stolen so many dreams.

'It was my job,' said *Russian* a while later in a low voice, as if talking to himself.

'Your job, right? Gimme a fucking break! Was it your job to double-cross people who trusted you? Was it your job to lie to them? To have them killed?'

'Oh please, don't give me that crap! You know very well that you did the same!' replied *Russian*, raising his voice and making two of the commandos turn to look in their direction. 'Or are you telling me that your rules did not demand you to do anything to win? I turned you in, but you were not killed!' he said, lowering his voice once again.

'I'm not sure what'd have been better.'

'Fact is that still you don't understand!' insisted *Russian*.

'Of course I understand, you motherfucker!' said *Rabbit*, losing his cool. 'Of course I understand! What about Marita, for example? Or do you mean to say that you had nothing to do with her death?'

'Nothing,' said *Russian*.

'I don't believe you.'

'Of course you don't believe me. You don't have any reason to believe me. But Marita was a useful contact. We had nothing to win by killing her. She was okay. Her views were a bit screwed up, it's true, but she was all right nevertheless. We could have gone very light on her.'

Rabbit could not hear any antagonism in what *Russian* was saying. The man was just being plainly objective. Probably more objective than he was being.

'There's still no reason why I should believe you, to me you're still the fucker who tipped them off about her,' he said, and *Russian* nodded. He didn't have to believe him, he added after a while. But if he listened, the story could look somewhat different from what he believed it had been.

And *Rabbit* chose to listen. He could have finished *Russian* on the spot. After all, he had been longing for it long enough. Surely the marines would have killed him, but that he was prepared to accept. In the end, though, curiosity won. He wanted to know how deep had the son of a bitch dug as a spy.

'Marita was the daughter of a military officer,' started *Russian*. 'He was a Colonel in the Administrative branch, sort of an auditor in uniform. The Army sent him packing in '73 after they found he'd done some mischief as Logistics officer of a Cavalry Regiment in Gualeguaychú. He ended up setting up a furniture business in Rosario, but it never came to much. I didn't know him. Marita seldom spoke about him and when she did you could hear her contempt, which I imagine extended to all things military. This is how she began fiddling with the Monta. You know the rest of the story.'

With that *Russian* fell silent. *Rabbit* waited, watching the frozen landscape as it emerged from the darkness. It was the beginning of dawn. As it got gradually lighter *Russian* picked up the story again and *Rabbit* saw he was speaking with his eyes closed.

'Marita was friends with many kids of the military,' he said. 'The first time I saw her was in the tennis courts of the Naval Club in Olivos.* She was there with her mother, who had already divorced the Colonel and was dating a naval officer. I was in the ESMA at that time and had already operated a few times with the cops.

'Then one night she was out in a dancing joint in Palermo with a bunch of friends when the place was raided. I was there too but she didn't see me and anyway I don't think she'd recognised me, for we had met only once. But I knew her right away and spoke with the guy in charge, an officer from the Federal Police. They were not there to make any arrests, they wanted the kids out because they had intel about a meeting of heavyweights in the neighborhood and there was a strong possibility that things would develop into a shooting.

'But you sure remember how it was with these procedures. Kids got wild, things got out of hand and you never knew what you could find. Usually we loaded everybody in a lorry and drove to the station to verify IDs. It was a slow process and altogether pretty humiliating, if you want, but with the practice the Orga had at forging credentials, there always existed the chance of finding something that didn't match, a tip that would take you to a heavier target.'

Rabbit listened carefully. The *Russian* spoke of things that in some way they had experienced from opposing sides. Now they were on the same side and a lot had passed off since then, but listening to *Russian* he felt nothing inside had changed. Their ideas were still at odds. Both were still attached to their ways of seeing the world. Both views were probably doomed, but that didn't change anything anyhow.

* Residential neighbourhood just outside the city limits, north of Buenos Aires.

Russian continued. 'They let her go after I put in a word for her, said she was just a stupid girl and she was Navy, but two days after that my CO called me to tell me that the police officer had informed him of my appeal. I spare you the shit he gave me. He wouldn't even leave my grandmother out of the list of losers that according to him had tried to teach me common sense. But he admitted that there could be something salvageable in the mess I had made by compromising the Navy's leadership, etc.

'In brief: his plan was that I would get closer to Marita and try to find out if there was something going on with some officers' sons that the cops suspected were involved in a series of petty robberies – cars' stereos, bicycles and the like – which they then traded for dope. None of this was the Navy's responsibility, but the argument was that these idiots were *our own* and everybody wanted to avoid showing the cops our dirty laundry.

'So I got to frequent her. A friend of hers was giving Yoga classes in her flat and I joined. You may remember her, I once introduced her to you. The mission got immediately more urgent once I discovered that both Marita and you had contacts with the Orga. I passed the information up and, from then on, the concept of the operation changed radically.

'But they killed her, nevertheless,' he said after a while, and *Rabbit* thought he could hear sorrow in his voice.

'Who did it?' he asked.

'I don't have a fucking clue.' *Russian* opened his eyes. 'The cops, the Triple A, the Orga, what difference does it make? Who knows, anyway? Everything was a mess, back then. It could have been anyone, but it wasn't us.

Marita was a very strong contact, a fantastic source of information. We needed her and her disappearing went against all our plans.'

Again *Russian* fell quiet and *Rabbit* took advantage of the pause to repeat that, anyway, he had been a son of a bitch. *Russian* turned his head. In the bluish light he seemed tired, almost old. He laughed sadly.

'Who wasn't, back then?' he asked. 'Were you a saint, uh? I'll say one thing, *Rabbit*: if I die here in the Malvinas, it's going to be a relief. I'd even ask you to kill me right now if it weren't for these blokes here who would fry you right away. But believe me, my life has been crap since all that shit began and I have no hope it'll get better. Ever.

'There's still much hatred and our side has been losing for quite a while now. The papers and most of the public opinion are smashing us because we tried to fix shit that is unfixable. It's in our insides. We are like this. In any case, we fucked up so many times that we no longer know who is to blame for what.

'If I make it back, no one's going to defend me or anything I've done. They will throw me to the lions just as they threw Marita out of the window. But my fall is going to be slower, more unpleasant, more controlled. They will make an example out of me, they will take pictures of me and tell everyone 'See here: see the way this wanker did it. This is not the way it should be done, we never asked for this.' And they'll pile on me every little inexcusable fuck-up still at large, as if my personal involvement had been crucial to them all. And you want to charge me with Marita too! You must be shitting me!'

He stood up. It was day now and it would have been foolish to stay there in the open.

'Maybe,' said *Rabbit*, putting an end to the

conversation.

'Let this at least be clear,' insisted *Russian*. 'I don't give a fuck whether you believe me, whether you mind or not whatever I tell you. I'm done checking my numbers. I don't need to apologize to anyone. We are all sons of bitches, each in his own turn. The matter is to assume it.'

He picked his rifle and instinctively checked the safety catch. Always elastic, without even caring to feel his legs or warm them up, he joined the section of commandos. Then, without a word, he took the lead and started to walk.

Even though he could admit that some of the things he had heard could be true, that didn't change *Rabbit*'s anxiety to avenge all those who had meant something in his life. Nevertheless, and although he couldn't see it right away, the conversation had fatally affected his longing for the satisfaction he felt he needed. Talking brings people closer. Killing requires a certain distance.

They had not gone more than a couple of hours when *Russian*, who marched in front, lifted a hand signalling to stop and fell to the ground. Immediately everybody followed suit. At a distance *Rabbit* appreciated as a little over 400 metres, a British patrol was progressing right towards them.

They had to move fast, it was a clear morning and impossible not to be spotted. At another hand signal of *Russian*, one of the commandos crawled to the right to secure the flank. The Brits did not see him, and when he reached the desired position he opened fire with three shots of his FAP.*

One of the Brits fell right away, but it wasn't clear whether he had been hit because all of them hit the deck

* Heavy automatic rifle fitted with a bipod.

at the same time. The surprise was now gone and *Rabbit* heard the commander of the enemy patrol shouting his orders as the rest opened fire.

He pressed the trigger a couple of times to see how the AUG responded and was surprised by the violence with which the recoil hit his shoulder. The Brits were firing like crazy and they managed to set up a MAG that began to fire tracer rounds. Standing up would have been suicidal, and it was clear that the enemy had located them because suddenly mortar shells began falling in front of them.

He could see no way out and thought that in the next moment he would be bombed to hell when suddenly an aircraft appeared from out of the blue and thundered over their position. It was a ground-attack Pucará and *Rabbit* wondered where it had come from. The Pucará passed at very low altitude and, with a tremendous roar, strafed along a line in front of the British patrol. *Rabbit* thought it was like when the cavalry arrives in the movies and enjoyed the accuracy of the shots that lifted the earth in front of him as if during an earthquake.

Encouraging his men with his sound arm held up, *Russian* got to his feet and ran ahead, shouting orders that the din made inaudible, but which obviously meant that they had to break contact. The Pucará returned to carry out a new wave of strafing over the Brits' position and, without waiting to be told twice, *Rabbit* began running like crazy. As he turned in the middle of his race he could see *Russian* who, still under enemy fire, stopped to pick up one of his men who had fallen.

After he had covered a considerable distance, he looked back once again. *Russian* was progressing slowly, with the wounded weighing heavy on his shoulder, and one of the commandos returned to help him. There was not a trace of the Brits, and he realised that they had either run away or else must be dead. But anyway it seemed that they had successfully broken contact.

The wounded commando had caught a bullet in his left ankle and was in extreme pain. He complained loudly and *Rabbit* thought that this was not unreasonable since the commando's foot hung onto the leg by just a strip of whitish skin.

When they finally stopped, *Russian* decided to try his luck and break radio silence. Someone eventually heard him, because a helicopter arrived that same evening. The men sought cover as soon as they heard the noise of the rotor-blades, but then they immediately realised that it was an Argentine aircraft.

Aided by the mechanic, they lifted the commando onto the chopper's deck and tied him in to prevent him from sliding around. *Rabbit* helped in the manoeuvre and, as he turned to exit the cockpit, found *Russian*'s rifle aimed at his chest.

'Sorry, *Rabbit*!' shouted *Russian* above the noise of the rotor. 'You're leaving too!'

He was looking at him without anger, without sarcasm, without anything that showed what his feelings were. In a moment he would never forget, *Rabbit* Aranda realised that his chances for revenge had been reduced to nothing, but at the same time he saw that it didn't matter any more.

Russian was destroyed and he had been able to measure the depth of his disappointment and dismay. He was a broken enemy, and maybe he was right in thinking his future would be an ordeal. He would gain nothing by killing him. The man was already defeated. For the first time and with no little bitterness he realised that that didn't mean anything either.

Out of pure anger, he shouted above the increasing noise of the spinning rotor-blades:

'I don't care! You're already dead!'

The chopper took off and he was able to see the hand raised in a salute. That was the last time he ever saw *Russian* Lovak.

You Cry Alone

This time he was not able to say no. It wasn't that he didn't want to go. The invitation was really tempting. For once they would be able to spend summer in a proper way instead of having to pester their summer-house-owning friends in order to allow the kids a rest from the heat of the city. Buenos Aires can be unbearable then, though it is lovely to stroll down its quiet, almost deserted sidewalks. The previous year, a series of blackouts in mid-January had hit several apartment buildings in the neighbourhood for as long as two weeks. It had meant no lifts and no AC, and the water supply had also been cut off.

Besides, he knew his in-laws longed for company. The beach house had become too big for them and it stood somehow isolated. It was far from downtown, on the way to José Ignacio and almost by the sea.

In any case he needed a rest. Indeed everyone was telling him that. He was at that point in life where everything seems to be centred on work. Dr Tomás Beltrame lived for his job. He couldn't have been able to tell who plain Tomás Beltrame was.

Silvia could also use some rest, she too worked too much and it was a long time since they had had time enough to talk together about things other than the immediate issues of family life.

They met when he was nine. She was six at the time and quite lively. She came every year to the beach along with her parents in mid-December and they rented a small house in San Rafael. It was always the same house, every summer, for a period of five years.

Once those summers ended, it took some time before he saw her again outside the Nursery rooms of the hospital where he was finishing his residency. By then she was a welfare consultant.

In '82 he was called up to complete his military service. He was twenty-three years old and not yet a graduate, but because of the impending war his appeal for a deferral was cancelled. His mother was beside herself with grief, but old man Beltrame was another thing altogether. Although he mistrusted the military, he held his – and everyone else's – civil duties in high respect, and did his best to show the optimism that he did not feel when they drove one damp morning up to the gate of the famed *Los Patricios* 1st Infantry Regiment where he would be billeted.

It was a tiring day for Tomás and his new mates. Assembled inside a warehouse, they did their best to sort out and pack the apparently excessive load of equipment the Army was issuing them, sweating like horses under the stare and hollers of a Sergeant called Zapata, whose use of language did not quite convey the sophistication normally associated with the Regiment.

Tomás couldn't make sense of the blunder committed by the geniuses in charge of recruitment. They had placed him in the same group as two other conscripts whose Christian names were Jorge and Bartolomé Tomás, and who had the same family name as his. To make things worse, Bartolomé Tomás was so used to his middle name that he would normally not answer when called by the first one.

Twelve days later, Alpha company boarded the aircraft that would take it to Puerto Argentino. Tomás' plane made a stop in Comodoro Rivadavia to load anti-aircraft ammunition and this resulted in the total weight of the plane exceeding the limits approved for take-off. Seeing this, the Major in command decided to leave five conscripts on the ground. Tomás was among them, but neither Jorge nor Bartolomé Tomás had the same luck.

From then on, troop transfers were suddenly restricted and Tomás and his mates remained stranded in Comodoro, where the director of the city's Military Hospital did not wait long to get hold of them and assign them to tasks within his own organisation. The hospital was managed as any other unit. The pace of work was maddening and all external communications were strictly regulated. Before he could even get a message to his parents telling them of his whereabouts, the Brits took Puerto Argentino, the Argentine troops surrendered, and he was discharged and sent home, just twenty days after the Company's survivors returned to the mainland.

Neither Jorge nor Bartolomé Tomás were among those who came back.

Tomás arrived in Buenos Aires very tired. Politely assuming that he had been through experiences he wouldn't want to remember, neither his friends nor his parents asked him anything. Argentina was bleeding through every pore and soon his role in the war ceased to be news. He considered the whole matter an awesome stupidity and without further thinking he resumed his studies. That same year he graduated as a M.D.

One rainy evening just as he was leaving the Hospital de Clínicas, he ran into one of his teaching assistants from the times when he was still a student and the man suggested they have coffee together as a way to catch up. Even though he was quite tired and anxious to get home, he agreed to sit for a while in a nearby bar. As they walked, trying to step over the loose tiles in the sidewalk, the guy asked him if he ever thought about the Malvinas. Taken by surprise, he only managed to say that the war had been a difficult experience.

The teaching assistant nodded in acceptance and went on to say that he had lost a brother in the war. The kid had been his junior and his untimely death had taken almost all the will to live from their parents. 'It shattered us all,' he said to Tomás, who listened in silence. He had seen some badly wounded guys at the hospital in Comodoro and witnessed the despair and disbelief of their parents. He knew how to respect pain.

'You too were called up, am I right?' asked the guy.

Again the surprise. Without really knowing why, Tomás felt ashamed of having been left behind.

'Yes,' he answered. 'But I was never close to combat.'

'Where were you assigned?' insisted the other.

'*Patricios*,' he said. 'Alpha Company, *Patricios*.'

The teaching assistant baulked. 'You don't need to say anything else' he said. 'You guys were in the oven from the very start.'

Tomás didn't reply. He knew that by not answering he was passively assuming the role of an impostor, but he somehow couldn't tolerate the idea of keeping this man from believing that he, who was as plain and uninteresting as any other Joe, was sort of special. On the other hand, he consoled himself, it was an insignificant white lie of no consequence.

'Many had it worse,' he conceded in the end. 'But I'd rather hear about you. It's been a long time since you last showed up here at the hospital.'

From that evening, Tomás began to consider the idea of having been on the Islands with greater ease. Without striving to jump into the same wagon of the ex-combatants for whom he felt more compassion than jealousy, he decided to let others assume what would have been normal to expect: that he had indeed been on the Islands; that he had somehow survived the tremendous psychological pressure of combat; and that he had returned more or less disappointed with little or no desire to be reminded of the experience.

As a result of their fortuitous encounter in the hospital's Nursery, he began to go out with Silvia and her group of friends. Most of them were still students and sometimes they would linger in the cafés near the University, discussing all kind of issues until dawn. As good *porteños**, every evening they were set to fix the world anew. When Tomás joined them he would sit in a corner musing silently, his hand on the nape of Silvia's neck as if showing off a trophy.

Then one morning, as they were coming out of a café on the corner of Corrientes and Talcahuano, she asked why he never spoke about the war.

'The guys know that you were there with the *Patricios*,' she said, referring to her friends that had just left. 'I think everybody in our class knows it.'

Once again he failed to deny it. He realised that by letting the delusion continue to live its life he was entering a trap from which it wouldn't be easy to get out, that he could get entangled in his own net. He told himself it wasn't important. The war had been a ridiculous mess anyway. He refused to discuss the matter.

'There's nothing to say about the war,' he answered, and Silvia chose to interpret his silence as the natural

* Born in Buenos Aires.

reluctance to recall a tragic experience. The love she felt for Tomás was genuine and did not need any incentive, but imagining him suffering silently from the pain and the trauma made her admire him. Her maternal instincts did the rest.

Three months later they were married and their first son was born within the year.

By then Tomás had already told Silvia the truth about his military service. He had confessed about it the night before they married because he meant to start on the right track and, although he still considered it an irrelevant subject, he realised that for Silvia it was not so trivial.

She was not particularly pleased to have him come clean. She felt disappointed. She knew that there was no reason to feel that Tomás was less of a man for not having fought actively in a senseless war, but somehow she felt cheated. For a long time she had thought she was marrying a hero. She now knew she was marrying a doctor. She was also bothered by the fact that he had hidden the truth from her for so long and had waited precisely until that moment to disclose it, like a bomb bursting in the middle of her bridal joy.

'It's unfair,' she said, and he realised that healing that wound would probably take him forever.

They were lying under the blankets and the moonlight shone through the open window. After a dreadful silence that seemed to last for an eternity, he felt her arm over his chest.

'This stays between us.'

'Okay,' he said, knowing immediately that he was making a tremendous mistake. But he didn't dare to lose her.

That evening he wasn't able to close an eye. Silvia

didn't either, but he never knew it. He didn't think a lot about it, but every once in a while he blamed her silently for having extracted that promise from him. He kept the deception and, though there were occasions when he felt like a miserable cheat, he eventually got used to the pretence.

Punta del Este bore a pale likeness to the pleasant resort he remembered and the new version disappointed him. The noise and the amount of people everywhere made it impossible to rest. Strolling one evening with Silvia and the boys along the main street, they stopped in front of a bookshop, and he decided to buy something to read on the beach. Knowing he would take some time, Silvia took the children across the street to buy some ice cream. He was about to step into the store when a small man carrying a parcel under his arm rushed by and pushed him to the side.

'I'm terribly sorry!' said the man, stopping in his tracks. 'Please excuse me, sometimes I can be so clumsy!'

'Don't worry, it's nothing!' answered Tomás, regaining his balance as he turned to walk on.

'Tomás?'

Tomás turned around, somehow startled. He knew that voice, it rang a bell but he could not remember where or when he had heard it. The man repeated the question, a little louder this time.

'It's you, isn't it? Tomás?'

'Yes, my name is Tomás,' he said, 'but I'm sorry, I don't know who you are.'

'You're one of the Beltrames,' said the little man, nodding to himself as if confirming a bet. 'You're the lucky one. And you don't remember me. Don't worry, I'm used to it, I also had trouble remembering many of them, for a while. Then they all returned to me almost at the same time. Not everyone, no. Some never came back. It is as if they had not only died.'

Tomás felt he was rapidly entering a state of general alarm. Who was this guy, how did he know his name and what did he want with him? He looked around, trying to locate Silvia, who was still queuing with the kids in the ice cream parlour across the street.

'Who are you?' he asked. 'Where do I know you from?'

'And you don't remember me, Tomás!' insisted the little man, smiling as if he was having a great time. Tomás realised his hands had begun to sweat.

'It is normal, or so say the doctors. But I do remember,' insisted the man, without looking at Tomás or at anything in particular. Tomás got the impression that he was talking to himself.

'I remember everything. I even remember the light!' He was moving away now, but was still muttering.

'Hold it!' said Tomás, stretching his arm in an attempt to get hold of the man's sleeve. 'Please tell me your name!'

Silvia was crossing the street now and it was obvious she had a question on her lips. The little man mingled with the people passing and disappeared.

'Who was that?' asked Silvia.

Tomás did not respond immediately, he was frozen.

'You look like if you'd seen a ghost. Are you all right?'

'It's nothing, I'm fine, really!' he reacted finally. 'It was just an old friend, an acquaintance, that's better. Forget it! He's gone now, anyway!'

They kept on walking in silence, followed by the kids, who were busy dealing with two over-sized ice cream cones. He could feel Silvia's irritation. She knew he was lying, but what could he say? That he had run into someone who shared the secret they had vowed to hide? It was better to try to remember who the man was and dismiss the whole thing as an unlucky coincidence.

The summer went on without other remarkable incidents but he could not forget the man who, without even knowing, had made him painfully aware of the simulation in which he lived. He could still hear the timid, intimate voice asking, 'It's you, isn't it? Tomás?' It gave him the creeps.

Then one evening Silvia's parents invited a couple of friends to dinner, Uruguayans who owned a ranch near the town of Rocha. Mr Mirández presently mentioned that he knew another farmer in the area, an Englishman who had fought in the Malvinas War and spoke with a certain nostalgia about the elation he had felt during those days, as if referring to a treasured and already gone era.

According to this man the Malvinas War had been fought in a fashion the world would probably never see again. It had been a confrontation of wills, where hatred born from atrocities committed or fundamental religious and philosophical differences had played no role. No matter how hard the commanders from either side had tried to demonize their opponent, almost every fighter on the ground or on board the ships and aircraft knew they were fighting a foe that was their equal in many respects, at least when it came to their notions of fair game and regard for human life. It was a weird thing, which in many ways had made the aftermath so difficult for many, because both sides knew they perceived the world in very much the same way.

Mr Mirández's friend also thought that the insularity of the conflict had had an influence on how it had been conducted. Modern warfare, he said, was so technologically laden that the loss of human life did not inevitably weaken the opponents. He thought the Malvinas War had been odd in that regard, for as the rivals were thousands of miles from any possible reinforcements, every soldier had been precious.

Mirández mingled dramatic pauses in his talk, letting each sentence sink into his audience as if he were submitting a declaration to a panel of judges. Everyone listened attentively, but suddenly Tomás realised that everybody at the table had their eyes on him as if waiting for his reaction.

'You were there, doctor. Isn't that right?'

'Yes, indeed,' answered Tomás with the tiniest hint of insecurity, as he tried unsuccessfully to think of a way out of the questioning he knew would follow.

'And what can you tell us? Was it so, as this man says?'

Tomás looked around trying to get support from Silvia, who instead of meeting his eyes left her chair to busy herself with the coffee service. Seated across him, Horacio lowered his gaze as if he had lost something under the table.

'Well,' he said finally. 'It's likely it was like that. I had a very short war myself, saw very little, almost didn't see combat at all.'

'I understand,' insisted Mr Mirández, 'but my friend's observation applies to all those who were there, no doubt. Would you say that it was a relatively un-cruel war?'

'I'm in the soup. I'll have to swim,' thought Tomás. He couldn't avoid the question without giving it at least a try, at the risk of disappointing everybody. On the other hand it was an easy question. One didn't need to have seen combat in order to give a reasonable answer.

'Cruelty is inherent in war.' he said. 'If what you mean is using unnecessary violence to make the other guy suffer just for the hell of it, then, and as far as I know, the Malvinas War was not a cruel war. But again, I saw just a tiny part of it.'

Mr Mirández seemed satisfied with the answer and, after further small talk, he and his wife stood up and thanked the hosts for a marvellous evening, lamenting that they nevertheless needed to go. It was a long drive back to their farm. Helping his wife to her purse, he touched once more on the war: '*Patricios*, I was told. You guys certainly had it tough!'

'Leave the boy alone, for God's sake!' said his wife, smiling warmly to Tomás. 'He's had enough bad luck already having gone through something so terrible, and yet here you come to remind him of it.'

Tomás was as white as paper. Was he being paranoid? Or was Mirández aware of his imposture? Was the man being polite? Or was there a tone of irony in his words?

'Excuse me, I think I need to sit down,' he said almost out of breath. 'The cold,' he added, and let the sentence die on his lips.

As soon as the guests were gone, Horacio offered him a drink.

'You don't look very well,' he said. 'You may be having a fit of low pressure. It was dumb of my friend to ask you about the war. It's an unfortunate lack of delicacy, but surely he did it with the best intention.'

'Don't worry,' said Tomás. 'I'm just a little tired. If you don't mind, I think I'll go straight to bed. I need to lie down a little.'

'Please do!' encouraged Eduardo. 'Take a good sleep

now and we'll see you tomorrow!'

When Silvia entered the bedroom a bit later he was lying on top of the bed. He had not taken his clothes off and he was staring at the ceiling. His eyes were wide open.

'You were good,' she said.

'He knows,' answered Tomás without looking at her.

'Don't be an idiot! How on earth could he know? He has probably no idea of what you were doing, and anyway it happened over twenty years ago!'

'I'm telling you, he knows,' he insisted. 'He knows and he was testing me.'

'Don't be paranoid!' said Silvia, unbuttoning her blouse and sitting at the side of the bed. 'It's impossible for him to know anything. You should forget it all and don't worry any more, these are only the ghosts in your head.'

He listened and accepted that perhaps she was right. It wouldn't have been the first time that his wife's common sense had saved him from losing his mind to an obsession. He decided not to worry, but he knew he would anyway. He was tired, but that night he didn't sleep.

The day they were due to return to Buenos Aires dawned cloudy and with a cold wind that made the kids say goodbye to the beach without regrets. They arrived at the airport on time and the plane was on schedule. As they were waiting to board, two men in civil clothes approached Tomás. With them was an officer from Airport Security.

'Tomás Beltrame?'

'Yes?' answered Tomás. 'Yes, I am Tomás Beltrame. Can I be of any use?'

The policeman spoke: 'These gentlemen here come

from the Investigations Bureau and would like to ask you some questions.'

'What?' jumped Silvia. 'Is there a problem? We're about to board a plane!' Tomás made some conciliatory remarks.

'Easy, Silvi!' he said as she fished for her mobile in her purse. 'It's probably nonsense, let me handle this and see what these gentlemen need! Keep cool and we'll soon see what this is all about!'

He turned towards the three men, who had backed up a little.

'Could you please tell us what you need?' he said, addressing the man in uniform. 'It is true that in a few minutes we have to board a plane.'

One of the men in civvies made a sign for him to come nearer, as indicating that he wouldn't speak in a very loud voice.

'Look, doctor,' he said, 'we have a problem and thought that maybe you could help us. A person was found dead yesterday evening and it is difficult to know whether it was a suicide or if there's something more sinister behind it. The reason we're here is that your name appears in some papers found in the apartment where the corpse was. It occurred to us to check the lists of people who left the country in these last few days and we saw you were leaving today. No need for alarm, this is always done as a routine procedure and may just be a coincidence. But we need your collaboration. I fear that if there really existed a relationship between you and the deceased, you will have to postpone your trip because we'd like you to identify the body.'

'Do you have a name?' asked Tomás.

'We have reasons to believe that the deceased was called Martín Cañizares. Does that name mean anything to you?'

'Indeed!' said Tomás after thinking for a moment. 'I knew him. We met in the military. But I don't think I could recognize him if I were to see him again. This happened many years ago.'

'Well, but you may still be able to contribute something,' said the other man in civvies. 'We know that he fought in the Malvinas War, and some of our people are now reviewing the documents he kept such as diaries, letters and other things he wrote. You don't have to worry about your flight. We'll take care of it and order new tickets. Would you rather have your wife and kids travel now? Or should we provide them with accommodation here for as long as you have to stay?'

'No, no, that's not a problem. But let me see a little here. We have commitments,' he answered as he turned to face Silvia, who was speaking on the phone.

He came closer and Silvia said in a low voice: 'I have dad on the phone. He says he can be here with another lawyer in twenty minutes. But we'll nevertheless miss the plane. What'd you want me to tell him?

'Let me talk to him,' he answered, taking the phone.

'Hi, Horacio! I thank you so much,' he said interrupting the questions that his father-in-law was making. 'I think this is not a serious problem, there's been a guy I knew who either has been killed or else blew his brains out and they want me to identify his body. It appears to be just a routine thing and they have asked me to lend a hand with their investigations.'

'They've asked you?' queried Horacio in an eager tone. 'Are you being asked, or do they require it from you? Do as I say, please! Ask them whether you have need for a lawyer and tell them you have me on the line.'

'Seriously, Horacio,' insisted Tomás. 'I don't think it

is necessary.'

'Just do me that favour, so that I may stay calmer,' answered Eduardo over the phone. 'And tell Silvia that if she decides to stay with the boys we're happy for them to come back. We will be here for one more week at the very least.'

Tomás lowered the phone. 'Will I need a lawyer?' he asked the policeman who was waiting for his answer. 'I have my own on the line.'

'No, doctor, by no means!' replied the man, offering him a smile that gave Tomás anything but reassurance. 'Believe me, it is just a matter of routine. We are not telling you to bring your wife because we can see that you also have your kids here. But this is completely harmless unless you have some strange story to tell us. Look, let's do this: if you feel more relaxed with a lawyer, bring one! I just say all this to save you from spending good money.'

'Sounds okay to me!' said Tomás. 'Then if I have the chance, I'd rather have my lawyer come. Can we wait here for twenty minutes until he joins us?'

The policemen looked at each other and shrugged. One of those dressed as a civilian said, 'Anyway, the bloke is already dead.'

'Go along and tell him to come, doctor, no problem!' said the other one. 'Tell him we'll wait for him here, in the departure hall.'

Tomás returned to the phone and told Horacio that they were expecting him.

'I'm on my way!' answered Horacio, and hung up.

Finally Tomás turned to Silvia, who stood staring anxiously at him. The boys played hide and seek among the rows of seats.

'We're staying!' he said, and could see she was concerned.

'It's nothing serious,' he reassured her. 'It's just a coincidence and it doesn't concern us. Cheer up, it has nothing to do with us!'

Shortly afterwards the Airport Security man came forward: 'Excuse me, doctor! If you think it's okay I'll have your luggage taken off the plane. Should we get also the lady's suitcases and the boys' duffle bags?

'Please do!' said Tomás. 'Here are the baggage tickets!'

He stroked Silvia's arm. She was obviously upset, so he pulled her closer to calm her down. All of a sudden he realised that the policeman had no way of guessing the type of luggage they carried unless security had been watching their movements from the minute they arrived at the airport. At that thought he too began to worry a little, for there had been already too many coincidences on the trip and somehow everything had a connection to that secret he kept trying to leave behind. To make matters worse, now even Horacio was going to be involved in this issue that threatened to bring to light the true role he had played in the war. 'Now that would really be unfortunate,' he thought. He was beginning to feel a headache.

Presently one of the policemen in civilian clothes approached him. 'This is of great help for us, doctor. We are very thankful. If we can put back together what happened it's going to save us a lot of work and money. Talking about money, as this is official business we are authorised to pull certain prerogatives and as soon as we're over we'll get you and your family on the first available flight to Buenos Aires. We always have them hold a few seats for us until the very last moment, in case an emergency shows up. Now let's wait for your lawyer and see if we can finish this within the day.'

Just as he had announced, Horacio arrived after twenty minutes with Sonia in tow. Sonia quickly took control of Silvia and the kids and they all left, having agreed that they would remain at the house waiting for the men's arrival. Tomás briefed Horacio on what he knew and the latter demanded to see the credentials of the policemen, who were in civilian clothes. Satisfied with the inspection of their IDs, they bade goodbye to the Airport Security man and one of the cops brought up a car with which he picked up the trio at the entrance of the building.

The car took them to San Carlos Hospital, where they parked and proceeded to the mortuary. The house's pathologist was there to receive them, a bald man in rimmed glasses who was well known to the policemen, or so it appeared to Tomás, judging by the way they bantered. Before entering the cold room, Tomás told Horacio that it was not necessary for him to join them.

When the pathologist removed the sheet to uncover the body, Tomás found himself looking at the face of the man he had run into at the bookstore's entrance almost two weeks before.

'Do you recognize him?' asked one of the policemen.

'Yes!' he said, only to recant himself immediately. 'No!' And then again: 'Actually, I know him, I've seen him before, but I have no idea who he is.'

'Could he be Cañizares?' asked the other policeman.

'Yes, he could,' answered Tomás, 'but he could be anybody else. His face doesn't tell me anything.'

'But aren't you telling us that you have seen this man before?'

'Yes, yes!' he explained, while the pathologist ran the blanket back over the corpse's face and pushed the stretcher into the freezer. He was trying to be consistent, but he realised the absurdity of the story he was trying to tell. They met Horacio again outside the cold room and he led the conversation as soon as Tomás had finished telling the cops about the incident at the bookstore.

'It is obviously nothing else than a coincidence,' he said, while trying to sound conclusive. 'There is nothing linking Dr Beltrame with the death of this man, you don't even know who he was. On the other hand, I was together with the doctor and his family all the time they were here in Punta del Este.'

'But you didn't not know about this bookstore thing,' said one of the policemen.

Horacio was about to reply, but the other cop took over and addressed him: 'Look, doctor, let's put things in black and white so that we can make some progress. If the doctor here' – he shook his head in Tomás' direction – 'knows something that can help us finding out how and why this guy died, we will be very grateful. Nobody is accusing the doctor' – another nod – 'of anything. There's not even evidence that this was a crime. We just want to close the file in the most tidy way possible, and if the doctor can help us to do it, then so much the better.

'You and the doctor are free to leave whenever you please. This identification was the only procedure that could have been extracted from him forcibly with previous permission from a judge, but that was not necessary thanks to his good disposition. Anyway, we are finished here. We will be pleased to notify the airport so' – he looked at the watch on his wrist – 'that they can take the afternoon plane. I think it leaves sometime around at three, right?' He looked at the other policeman who nodded in answer.

'Very well!' said Horacio, turning toward Tomás. 'Then we will be leaving you gentlemen! Do you want to take that flight?'

'No!' said Tomás, and Horacio's face changed from relief to astonishment.

'No!' he repeated. 'There maybe something else we can do to help solve this problem. Do you think it may be worth having a look at the apartment where he was found?' he asked. 'Did he live alone, did he receive any visits lately? Perhaps we may find something in the house that can clarify things a little more.'

The cops looked at each other without saying anything, but Horacio grabbed Tomás' arm roughly and took him aside. Without releasing him, almost upset, he hissed, 'Don't get into this! Think about Silvia and the kids who are waiting for you. Anything you say raises the suspicion that there is something weird here and you have something to do with it, and with good reason. You say you don't know anything about the guy, you are not even able to recognize his body and you are already asking questions. How do you know that he had an apartment, or a place, for god's sake? How do you know that they just found him as you assume, and that they were not... I don't know, alerted or something like that? Don't go on meddling in problems that are not yours. You have responsibilities! You have a name to protect!'

Tomás looked at the police officers, who were playing deaf to this exchange.

'Excuse us a moment please,' he said. He walked away a few steps with Horacio still clutching his arm and looking him in the eyes. 'I understand and appreciate what you're doing, believe me. But this is important to me. I get the feeling that if I don't get this clear right now it will dog me later. It's difficult to explain, I ask you for a little patience. I need to know what happened to this man. Who or what killed him. Why did he keep my name in his papers if it's already more than twenty years ago that I met him and I never saw him again? The meeting outside the bookstore may have been a coincidence, but I need to know if it really was mere chance or whether it was premeditated.'

'Okay,' said Horacio with reluctance. 'If you really feel like that, it's probably better that you go ahead and you got it off your back. But please be very careful with what you say! Remember that these blokes are trained to remember everything, absolutely everything.'

'You have nothing to worry about,' said Tomás as they approached the policemen. 'You've warned me, I've got it.'

'Let's go!' he said to the cops. 'Let's see what else we can find out!'

They parked the Volkswagen in front of a two-storey building in the outskirts of town. They entered through a side door guarded by two policemen in uniform and climbed the stairs up to a room with green walls. There was no other exit, the side door being the main entrance to that floor. Inside there was an unmade bed and several shelves with books, journals and notes in apparent disorder. A table with black iron legs and grey Formica top was pushed under the one window and there were two wooden chairs in front of it, the type one finds commonly in neighbourhood cafés. A fan with three dirty blades hung from the ceiling and several cobwebs decorated the corners.

Tomás entered, careful not to touch anything. 'May I touch?' he asked.

'Yes, there's no problem,' answered one of the policemen. 'Forensics has already been here. They took pictures and everything. They didn't find anything significant though, only some ID papers that included an Argentine passport. We sent everything to Buenos Aires for further research, but we still haven't received an answer. It's February, you see? Everybody's on vacation.'

'Was he found here?'

'Yes, right here. On top of the bed,' replied the policeman. 'He had opened the gas, it seems,' he added, pointing to a twin burner that lay in a corner, next to the sink. 'The newspaper kid realised something weird was happening as he smelt the gas. By the time we opened the door it was already too late because it had been four hours since he had died.'

Suddenly a stack of papers lying on the floor caught Tomás' attention and he took a sheet out of it in order to examine it more closely. The stack collapsed as he drew out the paper and he saw that some photos had been placed between the sheets, most of which looked like letters or loose notes. He lifted one. It was a picture of a group of fully-equipped soldiers and had been taken at the airport of Comodoro Rivadavia. It was the entire group of conscripts and the face of Cañizares was encircled in red.

'Here he is!' he said, showing the picture to the policemen. 'Martin Cañizares! I would have never recognised him! And here's me,' he added, pointing to his image in the picture. 'It was taken in Comodoro, when we went to the Malvinas.'

'Now this is puzzling!' said one of the policemen, looking at the back of the picture he had taken from Tomás' hand. 'Here on the back it has a list of names, but yours is mentioned three times.'

'An error, no doubt,' said Horacio, who had approached to inspect the picture more closely.

'If it's an error then there are two extra persons here,'

said the other policeman.

'It must be wrong,' said Tomás hurriedly, and grabbed the picture, placing it in his pocket.

'That's a piece of evidence,' the policeman said, extending his hand. 'So are all these papers here. They will help us to thoroughly clarify this issue. It seems to me that there's more here than what we're able to see at this point. I was told yesterday that the Argentine military attaché issued a special claim to extend his jurisdiction over all the evidence that we found.'

Tomás returned the picture and asked, 'Are we done?'

They went out onto the street in silence. It had started to drizzle and once in the car one of the policemen asked him where they wanted to be taken. Horacio gave him the address of the house and turned to Tomás.

'Do you want to travel now?'

'No,' replied Tomás. 'If it's not a problem, I would like to wait until tomorrow. Now I need to rest a little. I feel very tired.'

'It'll soon go away,' said Horacio. 'You shouldn't worry much about this.'

The policeman on the passenger seat turned around and looked at Tomás. 'Doctor, I want to thank you for your cooperation. As you surely know, to close a case requires some clarification as to the real name of the victim, the possible motives for a crime or credible reasons for death. With what you have told us, I think we have this case pretty packed in. Probably Cañizares entered into a deep depression that was exacerbated when you, without any malice, failed to recognize him. He then took the decision to take his life. This is normal in people who have suffered great trauma. I say this so that you don't feel guilty. These things happen and I understand that there were a few similar cases after the

Malvinas War, but you probably know more than us about that.'

They had arrived. Horacio said goodbye to the policeman at the wheel, asking if it was okay that they warned him a few hours in advance about the flight on which Tomás would travel.

'There's no problem, doctor!' replied the policeman. 'You have my mobile phone number. Call me and we'll reserve the seats as I said. Now you two have a good day and thanks again for the help!'

Tomás stood on the gravel, looking at the car as it disappeared around the corner, before he turned to follow his father-in-law into the house.

'You came just in time to join us for some tea and a roll of milk jam specially prepared with the help of the boys!' said Sonia, appearing in the kitchen door.

'Many thanks, Sonia,' said Tomás, opening his arms to hug Silvia. 'I frankly love the idea, but I'd rather lie down for a while if you don't mind. There have been enough strong emotions this morning and I'd like to be a little on my own.'

'I agree!' said Horacio. 'Take a couple of Aspirin and go upstairs, we'll be here and call you later! Don't worry about anything!'

'I really need to rest,' said Tomás, and Silvia nodded silently.

He climbed the stairs and found the bed still made, the unpacked suitcases at its foot. He approached the window and closed the curtains. He took off his shoes and leant on the bed, looking at the ceiling where the light that filtered through the seam of the curtains drew a very narrow wedge.

Then he realised he hated his life.

Changing Course

There was a chill to the afternoon and the pier cranes stood like lifeless flamingos against the sunset. Eduardo Mendoza eased slightly the jib's sheet and stabilised the boat to sail on the heading he wanted. Satisfied, he sat with his back to windward and lit the pipe he had filled minutes before the wind shifted. He liked to sail on the river. As a kid he had sailed on it with his father and he still felt immense pleasure every time he stood on the deck of a small yacht underway.

Over the port side, a bucket dredge blocked one side of the channel between buoys 4 and 6. It was a black and rusty structure and it reminded him of a prehistoric beast. A gust of wind announced the approaching twilight and he decided to change heading once again. He hauled the mainsail sheet until the boom was almost amidships and, as the boat came about, he dealt with the jib that was already flying in the wind. Then, as the hull leaned, he rested his weight on the gunwale, a hand on the tiller and the other holding the pipe.

'Easy,' he thought. As usually happened to him when sailing alone – and he sailed a lot on his own – he was soon invaded by the nostalgia of the intimacy he never knew with his son.

The black shape of the dredge began to fall astern and the horizon was now free for a starboard tack, but he resisted the impulse to ease the sheets and settled on a beam reach that would easily take him past Quilmes and to La Plata Channel, where almost all he remembered of his adult life had begun. He moved his body over to the other side and played to fluff the jib in each yaw that the waves imposed on the boat. The bow plunged like a knife towards the dark horizon.

He had graduated a Midshipman in December 1979 and three months later married Micaela, who had been his girlfriend from before he entered the Naval Academy. She was the daughter and grand-daughter of naval officers and presumably knew well what she was jumping into. But 1980 was not like any other year. Discontent in Argentina was on the rise, the military were seriously unpopular, and their salaries were a cruel joke.

Scarcely a month passed before she realised that keeping her marriage together was not going to be easy. Once the initial euphoria fizzled, she discovered that her husband had a dangerous tendency to let others think for him and that what she had previously admired as his sureness and firmness could be best described as well-concealed insecurity and automatic allegiance to a set of learnt and untested rules.

At the same time, Eduardo was full of qualms. He lacked diplomatic smartness and his postings were subject to the erratic strategy of the Navy's Bureau of Personnel. Failure to promote his interests, compounded with increasing economic strains, quickly overcame his attempts to impress his wife with the certainty and maturity he did not have. He barely knew her, a fact that was painfully obvious every time they argued. To add to his infirmities his father died, taking away a much-needed support.

Maintaining a status pretence was possible just because of the monthly allowance they received from Micaela's parents. Then, quite unplanned, she got pregnant. An untimely occurrence, for their difficulties

were growing. The humiliation of depending on his
wife's parents for support undermined Eduardo's pride
and his increasing obligations plunged him into a
complex arrangement of unpaid favours. Gabriel was
born one November night at the same time he, along
with six other men, was storming a meeting of the Orga
in the mezzanine of a stockings factory in Caballito.

Eduardo did not have a strong character, but military
training did its job, and he left the Naval Academy with
a deep instinct for survival and a clear sense of duty.
There he also learned to hate and to understand that
truth cannot be compromised. He loved his profession
and devoted most of his energy to work without asking
many questions, but it did not take long before he
realised that not everything he was doing was consistent
with the principles he had sworn to uphold.

This shook him deeply and he turned more and more
critical. Everywhere he looked he found reasons to
believe that the discredit piled on the military was
justified. It was not so much that he had lost his faith: he
felt he had misplaced it.

He was growing old, his waist was no longer slim, and
he began seriously to consider leaving the Navy. In those
days he had many arguments with Micaela. It was
obvious that they were both fed up trying to maintain the
act. He decided to distance himself and asked to be
transferred to Ushuaia. One Tuesday in early May,
fifteen minutes before six o'clock in the morning, he
boarded a naval Fokker in Ezeiza.* As he smiled to the
hostess, whom he recognised as the daughter of one of

---

* Ezeiza is Buenos Aires' International Airport, some 35 km
south-west of the city centre. Within its premises there
existed a Naval Air Station.

his former COs, the pilot called him into the cockpit. He was a Lieutenant with a boyish face. 'By your leave, sir,' he said, 'you're wanted on the radio.'

Somehow puzzled by the oddness of having to use the radio while the aircraft was still on the ground, he scanned the dashboard for something that resembled a handset before the co-pilot handed him a pair of headphones with a microphone attached.

'Captain Mendoza!' he said, donning the headset while the co-pilot pointed to a button on the dashboard. He pushed it, feeling terribly clumsy, and repeated his name. 'Captain Mendoza!'

'*Panther*?' he heard. '*Goat* here! A problem has arisen. You must disembark the plane. Come to my office, I'll be waiting!'

He removed the headphones, thanked the pilots and left the cockpit.

'Don't worry, sir,' said the pilot as he climbed down the ladder. 'I've already ordered your baggage to be taken down.'

He got off the plane, wondering what might have happened to make *Goat* Lima, who was the CO of the Naval Air Station, have him miss a scheduled flight. 'I'll have to notify Ushuaia,' he thought while he walked through the corridors, which were deserted at that unfriendly hour.

Goat sat in his office smoking a cigarette. He was a year older than Eduardo and they had not seen each other for three years when they had coincided somewhere in the Valdés peninsula during an amphibious exercise. *Goat* was a helicopter pilot and had had an emergency during an approach. The machine had hit the ground in an impressive way, but his skill had saved both him and the mechanic unscathed.

'Coffee?' he asked with a pale smile, as Eduardo came in. 'It's not worth it, but it's the only thing I have,' he added.

'You brought me here to offer me coffee? Come on, *Goat*, have a heart! I'm missing a plane!'

Goat pursed his lips. 'Please sit down, *Panther*!'

The tone of the order, almost gracious, told Eduardo that something foul was up and he wondered whether somebody had cancelled his orders. He reviewed mentally the details of a couple of JAG folders he had stashed in his baggage and knew were still pending, though not yet due. He was pretty sure they were still within the deadline for delivery.

'Is there anything wrong?' he asked as he let his body fall into the patent leather armchair that occupied a corner of the room.

Goat rested his buttocks on the front edge of his desk as he put out the cigarette in a glass ashtray that doubled as paperweight.

'This can be a shitty world, *Panther*! I just had a call from Micaela. Gabriel died this morning of an overdose.'

For a long time Eduardo would remember that morning as the last of his life. Or perhaps as the first one, depending on how he chose to look at it. Nothing, not even the war, had prepared him for this. The loss of his only son hit him like a steamroller and he became sullen, even aggressive at times. His bosses advised him to visit a psychologist. A few weeks later the advice hardened into an order and he was put on undetermined leave to undergo treatment.

He would sit silent in front the psychologist who interviewed him twice a week, a girl who could have been his own daughter. Now the Navy employed psychologists and this was a Lieutenant. 'This is a different Navy from the one I knew', he thought. Perhaps it was time to change course.

Then after a few months he was ordered to attend a conference in Mar del Plata. He decided to stay in town during the weekend, and on Saturday night he was having a drink at a bar called *Macao*, a place much favored by naval officers. After a while he began to talk with a woman. She was apparently on her own. She was interesting and smart, he told her he was a naval officer and she invited him to visit her father's shipyard next day. It was close to the fishing docks. He accepted and the visit lasted almost all Sunday, so at six o'clock he excused himself, saying that he had a bus waiting to take him back to Buenos Aires. The owner of the shipyard, an Italian by the name of Ruggiero, invited him to stay and take the first morning flight together with him because he also needed to be in Buenos Aires early.

Before Eduardo could answer, Ruggiero added that days earlier he had commented to a friend that he needed a new manager. This friend happened to be a Navy NGO and had mentioned Eduardo as a possibility, but the encounter he had had with his daughter at *Macao* had precipitated his plans. It had been an unexpected coincidence and he could not understand it as anything other than a good sign.

Eduardo was delighted, and before taking his leave he agreed to the conditions of the contract Ruggiero proposed and which they signed that very evening. He slept that night in a hotel which his new boss booked for him. The following morning before breakfast he left a package at the front desk, indicating that it should be delivered to the address printed on the label before noon. He also commissioned a huge bouquet of flowers and sent them with a crate of wine to the private address of NCO Alcides Vega, the instructor at the Diving School in Mar del Plata Naval Base who had mentioned his name to Ruggiero. He added a note in whch he invited his old subordinate to have dinner with him that week.

Satisfied, he sat down to breakfast in front of the ceiling-high windows facing the sea. He reminded himself that he would also have to locate *Goat* to reassure him that this is definitely not always a shitty world.

At quarter past eleven that same morning, a sailor seated at the front desk of the Navy's Headquarters received a postal packet that had already been inspected by Security. It contained an officer's cover, a sword and a note signed by Commander Dn. Eduardo N. Mendoza. Addressed to the Director of Naval Personnel, it read: 'Here I step ashore for good. Best regards.'

The afternoon was already dying. He gave good berth to the entrance beacons that guided the income traffic into Dársena Norte and – always mindful of seamanship – took down the jib before entering the anchorage proper, throwing the sail in the hatchway and leaving the deck clear for the manoeuvre. He steered the boat into the wind and came to the buoy almost with zero underway. Using a boathook, he fished the buoy cable and passed the bight through the chock before making it fast to a cleat amidships. Only then did he let go the mainsail halyard so that the cloth fell slowly, forming neat folds on either side of the boom. Then he pulled the pipe from his pocket and began to fill it as he watched the boats that floated peacefully over the dark mirror of the water.

'There's nothing like sailing!' he thought. 'Nothing!'

... and to The Lord His Dues

Patrick and *Bear* were waiting for him at the airport in Sauce. After the introductions, he climbed with his bag onto the back seat of the Land Cruiser and, as soon as they pulled away, the Scotsman asked him, 'Tell me, Eduardo are you also of the opinion that we should do something with the Islands?'

Catching the eye of his friend in the rear-view mirror, Eduardo thought that he had nothing to hide.

'See here, Patrick,' he said. 'I was done with the Islands in '82. They didn't matter to me back then and they still don't. I cannot for my life see what we could use them for and it seems to me that my country has more pressing problems to attend to. I fought because it was my duty as an officer, but I personally think that today the Malvinas would be ours had it not been for the war. I understand that you are behind some sort of project to help ex-combatants. That could interest me, because until somebody cares to put some order on the whole thing, their claims will only be helped by a few patriotic souls.'

Patrick did not speak immediately but held his gaze for a few seconds.

'There's a little more to it,' he said, making himself more comfortable on the seat, 'but don't you mind, we'll have time to talk about it in depth later. I guess that Nicanor – or *Bear*, as I'm aware that you call him – has already told you that we have a proposal to make. I say frankly that it's something I would have loved to do myself, but I lack the technical ability. Besides, I cannot neglect my interests here if we want this to go well. He told me much about you and, from what I heard, you seem to be the man for the job. But first we have to make sure that you and I speak the same language and share some ideas, wouldn't you agree?'

As he spoke the question, the Scotsman gave him another look. Eduardo thought the introduction had been a bit sudden, but soon discovered that it was enthusiasm that made Patrick address the matter so directly without beating around the bush.

'I fully agree,' he answered, and at the same time he realised that the Scot had asked only one question to assess his commitment. He was aware of his tendency to speak too soon and too openly and decided that he would be better off if for once it was him who did the scouting.

'So tell me, Patrick,' he began. 'I only know about you what the little *Bear* has told me: that you served with the Scots Guards on the Islands, that you were in command of the section that found Reche – who as I understand now works with you – and whom we had encountered a few hours before. But what is it that you're looking for with all this arrangement?'

'Let me explain it to you one step at a time,' replied the Scotsman, smiling as he sank deeper in his seat, 'for I don't really know what you are thinking about when you say "all this arrangement". I was a Sergeant in the Scots Guards, that is true. I enlisted in the Army when I was sixteen and joined the Regiment shortly before I turned nineteen. I was born in Glasgow. My father also served with the Scots Guards and fought the Nazis in Monte Camino. My grandfather belonged as well to the Regiment and was buried in a trench in Moval, during the battle of the Somme.

'So tradition weighs. Nevertheless, back in '83 I

retired from active service. I had seen enough: Malaysia, Sharjah, Northern Ireland and the Falklands. I had done my part. My wife had inherited some money, so we decided to buy this place and have lived here since. We managed to enlarge it and purchased some animals. Today we provide almost six percent of the milk consumed in Canelones and we export beef, mainly to Italy and England.

'In 1990 Nicanor arrived here and I trust you already know the rest of the story. By then, I had already been thinking about doing something in relation to the Islands.

'The current situation is a standstill, you see? We need to find a way to compensate the ex-combatants for what they did and at the same time put an end to the conflict that is still afoot. As I see it, the only ones who have benefited so far are the Kelpers, and they are still far from happy.

'Of course,' he continued, 'There are other opinions. Most Kelpers look at you Argentines almost as the French remember the Nazis. It may sound preposterous, but so it is. On the other hand Britain doesn't quite know what to do with them.

'And that's it!' he said. 'That is what I seek by trying to get you all in contact again with each other. I'd like to hear whether you guys are interested in helping me carry my plan forward. What do you think?'

Eduardo took his time to answer. He needed to do some thinking. The Scot seemed sincere and what he said made sense, but there was nothing there that really appealed to him. He was through with the Malvinas. It was more than that. He was through with forcing himself to be what he was not, with pretending to fulfil expectations that were not his own but those of the environment he had been brought up in. Until very recently, his story had been a path directed by the circumstances he had lived through, like a road that is built by the random laying of cobblestones and lacks a predetermined direction. He was no longer young. He did not want to waste time on causes that did not interest him. The effect they may have on other people he did not even care for.

Patrick returned to the attack. 'Both Argentina and the UK have associations that assist ex-combatants. Many of them promote businesses, loans, collaborations and mutual aid. In addition there are numerous examples of positive meetings between former combatants from both sides, but these initiatives are almost on the personal level and have a limited outreach. To get closer to our aim, Nicanor and I decided to establish an NGO to promote meetings of Argentine and British ex-combatants from any branch of the services, be they conscripts or professional military.

'We even set up a venue. We remodelled an old milking post, and hence established the Tumbledown Foundation. There are other friends, also ex-combatants, who wanted to collaborate as soon as they heard what we were up to. One of them is an old friend of mine, Javier Durham, who fought with the Paras. Javier retired from the Army in 1984 and lives in Montevideo. He owns a property on the Islands, more precisely on Wedell Island, the one you call San José. Another associate is my brother George, who lives in Plymouth but spends half the year in Punta del Este. George is a former officer in the Royal Navy who saw action at sea off the Islands and the Gulf before retiring from active service. There is also Archie, our finance guru. He is another former fighter who also lives in

Montevideo. Between him and my wife they look after what we might call the logistical aspects of the Foundation.

'Now all that is very well, but here comes the interesting part,' he said, taking a respite, 'Burren Glenn, the property that Javier owns on the Islands, is quite large. It has a house, a shed and some pens. Most importantly, it is prime land. On top of this, Javier has good contacts in Stanley and knows the Kelpers quite well.' Patrick paused and sunk again in the seat, facing forward. *Bear* found Eduardo's gaze in the mirror.

'So what do you think, sir? Now you see what we are up to?' He turned his eyes back on the road and Patrick spoke again, this time without turning his head.

'It's simple,' he said. 'We want to exploit that land through the Foundation and channel the profits to the respective associations of ex-combatants. The general idea is to distribute the profits in equal amounts between Argentine and British associations, even though we are aware that this may not be the best in some cases. But we think it is more impartial, anyway. We are counting on retaining ten percent of the revenues to finance the operation.

'But of course there are some risks. I would almost say that the plan requires that we act as military, that is why I was interested when Nicanor explained to me the way in which you had operated and the cohesion that the group had achieved. In addition to speaking very well about you, he said he could get you guys together once again, if needed. I do not know how much you know about the current situation on the Islands, but there are people for whom our intentions may not be good news and therefore we need a very solid team.

'The idea is to import cattle from here and start

breeding and slaughtering it on Burren Glenn, and then pack it there for export. Neither the Islanders nor the Argentines or the United Kingdom have to be able to extract any profit from the enterprise. The argument is that the production will take place in a territory that we believe is still in dispute and where no one can therefore enforce customs duties. The duty costs of exporting the livestock from Uruguay is an expense that will be covered by the Foundation, but that is a neutral tax, if you understand. The central idea is to ensure the participation of ex-combatants into the possible economic exploitation of the archipelago, you get it?' he asked, turning around to better convey the point.

'Yes, I get it,' answered Eduardo. 'I get it and I think you guys are crazy. As I already told *Bear*, I think it's a droll idea.'

'Not so droll,' said Patrick, turning briefly and pausing.

'Not so droll,' he repeated. 'We've been working on this for over two years now. You see, in 1988 Javier showed me a study that a team of researchers from the University of Buenos Aires did on his property. It was done before the war, and it was carried out by a team of American and Scottish scientists, working together with technicians from INTA*. The whole thing was sponsored by FAO and revealed a micro-climate centred somewhere south-east from Kelp Creek, exactly on top of Burren Glenn.

'The researchers installed an experimental station and discovered thicknesses of humus that are unique to the archipelago. They recorded the regimes of winds,

---

* Argentine National Institute for Farming and Stockbreeding Technology.

temperature and rainfall and the slope, speed and flow of the creeks that run into the valley, as well as the quality of fresh water found at different depths. In short, a very complete survey that spanned five years and was presented at a FAO Conference in São Paulo, where the sponsors proposed using the place for experimental production of beef cattle. In 1996 Javier made the property available to the Foundation.

'The idea of doing something that circumvents the ambitions of both countries and the Islanders is neither new, nor did it occur only to me. We will surely touch upon this later and in greater detail if you wish, but let me bore you a little more today while we share a few *matés* in the house, for we are already there.'

Indeed, after crossing a cattle grid they reached a rough wooden gate that served as an entrance to the property and a large one-storey house revealed itself behind a row of eucalyptus. A huge wisteria hung over its door. Once inside they sat in the living room, facing a coffee table that looked like the drumhead of a kettledrum and was covered with a thin glass top.

'It's the drumhead of one of the Scots Guards ceremonial drums,' explained Patrick. 'It was a present the Regiment gave to my father.'

'I'll set the water for the *maté*,' said *Bear* as he tossed a wedge of *quebracho** into the fireplace where a few embers had been left burning.

'It all began in '89,' said Patrick. 'I was in New York visiting a friend who was working for UNDP in Belize. One afternoon, I cannot remember why, we both realised that as a rule combatants fail to get much out of the wars they have fought in. As a fact, they normally are the first

---

* *Schinopsis lorentzii*, a very hard wood tree.

everyone wishes to forget about. A clear example of this was the attitude of the Thatcher administration towards the Falklands combat veterans. Also, you know about the suicides and all that. Months after that conversation, my friend called me to suggest we met with some people he knew in the UN and who were interested in knowing what had happened after the war.'

Bear reappeared from the kitchen, balancing a tray with a *maté*, sugar, *yerba* *and an iron kettle, and Patrick paused to welcome him.

'Thank God you're here,' he said. 'If it were for my manners we'd die of thirst!'

He blew into the *maté* before filling it with *yerba* as he continued. 'These people were UN officials and liked the idea of supporting an initiative which would benefit ex-combatants, as an initial step to solving a conflict that already then was kind of an embarrassment.

'Among them were representatives of England, the USA, Spain and several South American countries. All – or nearly all – of them agreed that there was much to be said for the idea of finding a solution outside the official circuits. That way the political and national differences could be downplayed and things could be focused primarily on the needs of the ex-combatants. They commissioned me to propose a project that could make it happen.

'I returned to New York in due course with a sketch of the operation. Soon the persons we had spoken to began to lobby Argentina and Britain to give a green light to the initiative, which although not related to their claims could help bring out the goodwill everybody knows has always existed between both countries.

* The herb used to make *maté* infusion.

'After much talking, it became clear that those who were the most opposed were the Kelpers, who claimed sovereign rights over the territory and its entire potential yield. Thus the operation we intend will have its risks, because we're going to press their thumbs while neither Argentina nor Britain will agree to raise the tone of the dispute and make new enemies by bailing us out.'

'What do you think, sir?' asked *Bear* once again, grabbing an armchair and sitting on it. 'Doesn't it sound interesting?'

Patrick busied himself with the *maté*.

'I'm awfully sorry,' he said, 'but I cannot really control my verbosity when I sit down to discuss this matter.'

'Don't worry' replied Eduardo. 'I like what you say, although I don't understand very well why you need us. I know nothing about cattle.'

'The operation requires a well-oiled team,' said Patrick, 'but there are also security issues. We need a group of smart and determined people.'

The evening grew as they chatted. Patrick did most of the talking, mixing anecdotes about how he had developed the project, details of the Foundation and the support that the initiative had generated from everybody he had shared his idea with.

Eduardo learned that the project was already quite advanced. George, Patrick's brother, had been working for the last twenty days in a shipyard in Tigre. Along with other veterans who would be part of the crew, he was busy modifying the fishing vessel that would be used to transport the livestock. There were still some details to address, but everything was more or less in place already.

It was time for him to make a decision.

Bear was familiar with Eduardo's times so he didn't

press his friend further. They left Patrick and when they arrived at his place he allowed Eduardo to ponder quietly in front of the fireplace while they shared a bottle of wine without coming back to the subject. They were both tired and withdrew early.

Eduardo dreamed that he was in a cage. It was huge and very comfortable and he couldn't make out its boundaries, but he knew it was a cage.

The Meaning of Goodbye

They found Patrick enjoying a breakfast that also awaited them. They sat at the table and soon after Eduardo said, 'I'm afraid I don't have good news for you.'

He took a drink of his coffee and smiled at the Scotsman, who looked at him without batting an eye.

'After giving it much thought I have decided to decline your kind offer. I honestly appreciate your trust very much as I do *Bear*'s when he suggested I could be useful. Your project is really interesting, but it's not for me.

'I'm into something else now. My current life has nothing to do with what you are proposing and, to be sincere, I have lately been trying to put everything that has to do with my past as far back as possible. I really want to have a fresh start.'

The Brit looked at him blankly and Eduardo felt he needed to explain further if he wanted to make himself clear.

'Patrick,' he said, 'you too are a former soldier. It's possible that we don't see eye to eye, but you will surely understand if I say that what led me to fight was the loyalty I owed to my men and the Navy, to both of whom I was always committed, independently of the cause we were fighting for. I had a duty towards them and I honoured it. But now I don't have that duty any more.

'In some lucky cases this loyalty turned into friendship as with *Bear*, and it makes me very happy that we continue to see each other and develop the bond we have, but once each of us retired from the Navy we chose a new path and followed our own interests. I admit that at first I was tempted by the idea of working together once again. For a moment I almost believed it could be possible to recreate what we once had. But life isn't like that. That was a terrific period in our lives but I really think one cannot rewind and make things happen again, and I don't want to spoil the memories I have by trying to recreate those days. I don't want to look back. The Malvinas is a part of my life of which I am very proud. That's all it is. Today it's not my life any more, nor my cause.'

'And the veterans?' asked Patrick

'They're just what they are,' answered Eduardo. 'Or what we are, better put. Some are called Pedro, others Juan, others Eduardo. We are common blokes who happened to share a unique experience more than twenty years ago now. One that was terrible to some, frustrating for others and maybe enriching to few. But their lives go on. They didn't stop with the Malvinas.

'Look at yourself!' he continued. 'Malaysia, Ireland, the Falklands? Haven't you also put a brake on the processes they might have started in your mind? Have you not closed those chapters too? Think about it a little bit. Is it really that important for you that the kelpers appear to be the ones with the lion's share? Hasn't it always been like that? The dog that watches while other dogs fight for the prey is the one that ends up eating while the others are busy licking their wounds. There is nothing new in that. It's an unwritten law! We can agree that the current efforts to help those whose lives were seriously screwed up by war are not efficient enough or are badly managed, but that is a matter for governments to care for, they have the means and from them we expect this kind of support. And of course it bothers me when they do nothing, just in the same way that many other shortcomings that have nothing to do with the war piss me off. So you said it very well before: I am a former fighter. I do not fight for the Malvinas any more. Now I just try to re-build my life.'

He paused, and they ate in silence.

After a while, as another round of coffee was being poured, Patrick spoke. 'Thank you, Eduardo! I am indeed grateful for your honesty. I understand what you've explained and extract two conclusions. The first is that you don't share the sentimental approach that often dominates your countrymen's relation with the Islands. I don't know the reasons why you react differently in this sense, but it shows objectivity that I personally consider healthy. The second is that you value and respect the memories of your time with the combat divers in a way that is only possible when an experience has been really important, and you want that memory to remain intact. Am I mistaken?'

'Please continue,' encouraged Eduardo.

'This leads me to think that perhaps Nicanor and I did indeed overestimate the effects of getting the Toritos together once again. But as you will surely understand, I'm a businessman and it's not for sentimental reasons alone that I want to succeed in this. There are other, more practical, reasons that make this operation interesting. Let me ask you what would you have answered if my offer had been made without me mentioning all the factors I have revealed?'

'That's easy,' answered Eduardo. 'If you'd offered me to make ready and sail a ship loaded with livestock from A to B, the only thing that would have concerned me would have been agreeing to a figure and concentrating on the possibilities to turn this stint into a permanent engagement. As you know I'm trying to secure myself a new job that I like very much and which I hope will last for at least the next fifteen years, and it just wouldn't make sense leaving it now to go and play master mariner for a couple of months. That means that probably I wouldn't have accepted anyway. On the other hand, even if I had decided to accept, it would have been under the condition that I'd be given a free hand to select my crew from among people with whom I have sailed before.'

'And you, Nicanor, what do you make of what your Lieutenant here says?'

Bear placed his mug on the table. 'I must confess to you both that I just realize how true all this sounds.'

'How true what sounds?' asked Eduardo.

'Well, what you're saying. That it cannot be, that you are no longer Lieutenant Mendoza and I am no longer *Bear* and none of the others is probably any more the way we remember they were. That one cannot remain chained to what it once was.

'When we began planning all this, the veterans issue was weighing a lot on my mind. All the injustice, the useless sacrifice and that entire story you know as well as me. But it's all a deception. Life goes on, and if nobody cares, it may very well be that it is time to accept that nobody cares, as simple as that.

'But then I was so revved up that I really came to believe we were going to be able to recreate what we had in the Malvinas and it seemed a good idea to propose to the group. However, it is as you said: the group, even if everybody shows up, it will never be what it was then. Now we are only friends at best, we are not even sure of having anything in common besides what we lived together. And that happened almost twenty years ago.'

Patrick stood up and addressed Eduardo. 'You guys

have not left me with much to say,' he said with a listless smile. 'I'm not going to have you waste more time. I understand and respect your point of view. I think that we can agree that both Nicanor and I got a bit carried away by our enthusiasm and this was perhaps not such a good idea after all. But then let me ask you a favour before you leave us.'

'Certainly!' said Eduardo.

'The matter is as follows,' continued Patrick, as they met the blaze of the morning sun outside the gallery. 'I will most probably be able to find another captain soon. That shouldn't be a problem given the current employment rates within the trade, but it is certainly going to take me a few days. Nevertheless, I need to complete the crew now and start immediately with the sea trials. It is a matter of three or four weeks, but it is a matter of haste for us. If you were willing to take care of that and then sail the boat to Montevideo, I'd appreciate it a lot because I really don't have any other solution at hand.'

'But didn't you say your brother was already on board with his people?'

'Yes he is, but he is still missing a few critical crew members. You'll see when you to talk to him, if you decide to go for this. In addition, despite being a former naval officer and having a valid sailing licence, he has no Master Mariner's licence, that I understand you do have. Of course, we would put all this into a formal contract.'

'If we are talking about a month then I've no objections.'

'Excellent!' said Patrick, smiling to show how pleased he was. 'Let's then look forward to this afternoon's meeting where you will meet George and see your friends once again. The idea is that the boat should be ready for trials in the coming week.'

Shortly after eleven o'clock, *Tony*, *Numa* and *Wizard* arrived in a double-cabin pick-up truck, filthy with dust from the road.

"Morning!' *Wizard* greeted José Reche as the latter approached them. 'We're looking for Mr Contreras.'

'You're looking for *Bear*?' asked Reche, who had already recognised the angular, dark face.

'We're here!' said *Wizard*, turning to *Numa*, extending his hand to Reche. 'Precisely.'

'The name is Quispe. Nice ranch you've got there!' he added, nodding toward the house that could be seen through the row of trees.

'It ain't mine. It's his, here.' said Reche, nodding in Patrick's direction as the Scotsman approached to greet his guests.

'Let me welcome *the Toritos*!' said Patrick, startling the newcomers.

'*The Toritos*?' asked *Wizard*, narrowing his eyes in a smile, and well aware that the man was a foreigner, for Patrick spoke with a strong accent. 'Maybe we've met already, sir?'

'No, we haven't, but I know your story,' said Patrick, stretching out his hand. 'Of course you don't yet know how, but I promise that all mystery will be gone once *Bear* explains. My name is Patrick McCloggey and, as Pepe said, that over there is my house and you are my guests. On the other side of that low hedge you can see Nicanor's house. Or *Bear*'s, if you prefer. But please follow me because they're waiting for you! I guess that you are conveniently hungry, right?'

Wizard parked the van and they filed to the house as *Bear* and Eduardo came to the door. Suddenly the morning was filled with laughter and mutual exclamations of surprise until they all got into the house, where soon a *maté* round, not unlike those they had held many times before, was initiated.

Listening to his friends exchanging stories that had not lost their lustre despite everyone present knowing them by heart, Eduardo reflected on how good it felt to be together once again with these men to whom he would gladly trust his life. He could certainly recall the tough times but, all in all, he was extremely fond of them and felt a singular pride, realising that even now, when the difference of rank had no more meaning, they still offered him the deference and loyalty of yesteryear. He told himself he would go all the way again if he was given the chance.

It was his turn with the *maté*, but he managed to get the attention needed to pass on the news.

'Guys,' he said, '*Bear* and Patrick have an idea and think that we can help them.'

'And so?' asked *Numa*, 'are you finally going to tell us about it?'

'You haven't changed at all!' replied Eduardo, amused with *Numa*'s impatience. 'Not for the better, at least. Can't you see I've just began to talk?'

'Let the boss speak, you dummy!' said *Wizard*, giving *Numa*'s shoulder an affectionate punch.

Eduardo explained the project as best as he could and then fell silent, waiting for his friends' reactions. *Numa* listened anxiously as was his habit, wanting to get ahead on the details as soon as he had made up his mind. He was a sucker for data, rapidly memorising numbers and names. *Wizard* listened attentively, but his face did not show anything. In that sense he was as readable as a statue and it was impossible to know what he was thinking. *Tony* stirred the straw inside the *maté* and kept silent.

'I'm in!' said *Numa* presently.

Everyone looked at him.

'Am I the only one?' he asked with surprise.

'We don't know yet,' answered Eduardo. 'For my part, I am determined to participate in the first phase, which will mean going through the reception of the ship as soon as the shipyard is done working and sailing her for the sea trials. That's going to take about three weeks and the idea is to begin as soon as tomorrow. Then I will return to what I'm doing now.'

'What about what follows, the rest of the operation?' asked *Numa*.

'No. For the rest I will not be in and I can explain to you all why, but the fact remains that I've decided not be part of it.'

'And you expect us to go along anyway?' asked *Tony*, who, up to that point, had not uttered a word.

'Nobody expects anything, *Tony*,' said *Bear*. 'It's just an offer, a job offer, if you want.'

Tony's concern touched a fibre in Eduardo's heart, making him appreciate that his friends had a right to share his whole view of the situation as he had explained it to Patrick and *Bear*.

'Look,' he said, 'it's possible that you guys are a bit confused about why we have gathered to listen to a proposal that is really an individual offer. The assumption was that we would all accept it right away, but I chose to reject it because I believe that, although we are very good friends, we don't operate as a group any more. Each of us has his own interests and knows the way he wants his life to be, plus each one of us has assumed private responsibilities that the others may not know about. I simply believe that it would not work well.

'I never asked you guys for your opinion about the Islands or the ex-combatants, and I don't even know if we agree in those views. Thirty years ago we were not only younger but we shared a vision of things. We lived inside the Navy and each of us adapted in his own way. Although today I can't meet you without remembering those days, we are different people now. The *Toritos* are history, what we did is history, and now we take our decisions thinking about other things than the group.

'I have a life planned elsewhere. *Bear* lives here. You, *Wiz*, are in Río Turbio and have made your life there, while *Tony* and the recruit' – he turned to *Numa* with a smile – 'walk Madryn, as they have always done. It's for you to choose. For my part I don't want to have anything else to do with the Islands. I don't owe them anything and they don't owe me anything either and, more than a former combatant, I like to define myself as a former naval officer.'

For a few minutes the group held the same silence they had observed during countless *maté* rounds in the middle of nowhere, on secluded beaches, in the darkness of the jungle or in the unforgiving cold of the Islands. Those had been other silences, though: moments when each of them day-dreamed on their respective days to come, longing for their loved ones or for past moments of particular happiness. Now they were closing a chapter. In the end, it was *Wizard* who spoke for all.

'It was good with the *Toritos*,' he said. 'It'll never be better.'

Touching Heaven

Tony and *Numa* arrived in Tigre after setting their private affairs in order. It would be a long absence, as they had decided to make the ship their home for as long as they were part of the operation. What for *Tony* meant a temporary solution to his chronic lack of direction, to *Numa* was an opportunity to add yet another interesting adventure to his backpack.

Assisted by a few hands from the shipyard, *Rosamaría* left her moorings on a quiet sunny morning and, at precisely nine o'clock, entered the Paraná de las Palmas where the river pilot said goodbye and boarded the pilot boat. Once the craft was clear from the side, Eduardo ordered starboard helm and the ship entered Mitre canal, keeping close to the green buoys.

As Eduardo had chosen to load in Dársena Norte at the docks permanently assigned to the Navy in order to reduce draft when sailing from up river, the ship was sailing high on the water. On reaching the junction with the Main Access canal, he took another turn to starboard, giving good margin to the bucket dredger operating near the Km 7 Beacon. At half past twelve *Rosamaría* moored beside the dry dock and, at five in the afternoon, she was loaded and ready to sail.

The stowage had been planned in advance by George and he had distributed the load in all possible places, for the idea was to ship as many animals as possible on the first voyage. During the trials, though, real navigation conditions were simulated by the use of sandbags. Their total weight was precisely calculated to simulate the livestock for which they would be replaced once the vessel arrived in Montevideo.

Once everything had been double-checked and deemed seaworthy, *Rosamaría* sailed as the sun began to sink behind the city skyline. As arranged with Patrick, Eduardo's intention was to take advantage of the three days of trials contracted with the shipyard to verify not only the performance of the repaired engine and the two new propellers, but also to assess the behaviour of the major changes done to the vessel's topsides.

Already in the outer anchorage, the ship sailed past the narrows at Banco Chico and emerged in the Middle canal. The sun had already sunk when they rounded the Codillo and set course to the east under a clear but moonless night. The tall smokestack of Quilmes refinery was clearly visible on the port quarter and an orange glow betrayed Montevideo on the port flare. A little more toward the bows, the lights of Recalada Pilot Boat disappeared under every other wave.

Eduardo decided to change helmsman and, as there was little traffic on the canal, he increased the vessel's speed to twelve knots. The deck rolled under his legs and he repeated to himself that he didn't know of any sensation that could match the attentive silence of a ship's bridge during night-time navigation. While he enjoyed the return to what he considered his natural habitat, the new helmsman appeared on the bridge followed by the Master's butler, the latter balancing a tray laden with several mugs and a pot of coffee.

'How are things going below?' asked Eduardo without removing his eyes from the bows as he took a mug and thanked the butler with a nod.

'Couldn't be better,' replied the butler. 'Everything works as smoothly as if we were back in the Navy.'

'That's okay,' said Eduardo, 'only that this time it can be still more fun and the pay will certainly be better.'

'I actually wanted to talk to you about it,' said the butler. 'Would it be possible for the men to learn a bit more about this livestock thing? I had no idea that one could raise cows in the Malvinas! Taking them down there is very interesting, but some of us would also like to know whether this is a one-off or otherwise, because maybe we can look forward to other trips of this kind.'

The sailor who had by now been replaced at the wheel joined in. 'Seriously, boss, the job is fun and pays well. But it would be good to know how long it'll last as well as more details of the operation. Maybe there is even something else we can do once we know the purpose of all this, don't you think?'

'Don't worry,' Eduardo reassured them. 'As soon as we are through with the trials we're all going to have a meeting about this in Montevideo. The owners and the new captain will be there and they'll reveal the whole plan. But let us first finish assessing the boat's seaworthiness to see whether the operation is at all possible.'

The sea trials were satisfactory. *Rosamaría* responded well and the engines kept the steady rhythm typical of well-tuned mechanisms, showing normal consumption values. The crew knew well what they were doing. Everybody received the proper training in damage control and, under George's supervision, hull-fittings and bilges were verified repeatedly with nobody finding anything unusual during the whole passage. Up on the bridge, three sailors took turns on watch every four hours along with Eduardo, George and *Numa*, who was already up to date with the systems and equipment on board.

In his free time, Eduardo trained *Tony* on some navigation basics to prepare him as a backup DO* and a couple of times, in open waters and with the horizon clear of vessels, he left him alone on the bridge. He also made sure that the boatswain was capable of replacing the helmsmen in case one of them had to be temporarily taken out of the duty roster. Four days after sailing from Tigre, *Rosamaría* moored at Pier B in Montevideo, well sheltered behind the inner breakwater.

Patrick, *Bear* and Archibald Towney were waiting at the pier next to the new captain, for Eduardo had alerted them by phone upon entering the channel. Once the docking manoeuvres were finished and the gangway set, they all went on board and toured the ship, guided by Eduardo and George, who explained in detail each of the modifications done while in Tigre and expanded on the results they had produced. The new Captain appreciated the changes and the quality of the new equipment that had been installed and, when the tour ended, Patrick proposed to gather the crew and introduce them to the new Master, clarify any possible doubt about the voyage they were embarking on and explain other details of the operation to those who were still not quite clear about its ultimate goal.

There were no surprises. At Eduardo's behest, Patrick gave the crew all the information they requested. As he had hand-picked seven of the crew members without any conditions from Patrick, he couldn't help but feel anxious about how they would react once they heard about the true nature and scope of the project. But at the same time he knew he had chosen well. All of them were

* Duty officer.

good professionals. They had served at sea during the war and liked the idea of sailing with a different purpose than just making some money.

That same night *Wizard* arrived in Montevideo, driving one of his trucks. His plan was to enter the harbour through the Florida Gate, attracting as little attention as possible, because the less people who knew about the operation, the bigger the chances were of the cargo reaching the Islands safely. Also this would make it easier to delay the inevitable reaction of local organisations that opposed the venture. Through months of incessant lobbying the Foundation had made sure that both the British and Argentine authorities would do their best to avoid sticking spokes into the wheel, but the reaction expected from the Kelpers was not so encouraging.

It was almost twelve o'clock when he arrived at the gate and the Customs booth was closed. Despite this there was a Coast Guard sentry guarding the entrance. As the truck stopped the sentry got up from the stool he had been sitting on and approached the driver's door with obvious reluctance.

'The gate opens at eight o'clock!' he said. And a bit later, realising it was a Saturday, he added: 'On Monday!'

Wizard opened the door and jumped down from the truck's cabin. It was cold and there was almost no traffic on the Rambla, the ample boulevard that runs along the coast separating the beaches from the city proper. He pulled a packet of cigarettes out from his pocket and offered one to the sentry. The man's eyes scanned the surroundings hesitantly before he stretched a hand to take one.

Wizard offered his lighter.

'Cattle?' asked the sentry, nodding towards the trailer

as he lit up.

'Heifers!' answered *Wizard*. 'Livestock! Uruguayan!'

'Where are they going?' asked the sentry, getting more talkative now.

'To Tierra del Fuego.'

The sentry cocked his head. 'Is that so? Fuck no!'

'Don't you believe me?'

'How could I? To Tierra del Fuego, you say! They're going to freeze to death out there! Also, there are no cows there at all!'

'Who told you that there are no cows in Tierra del Fuego? I believe there are.'

'Not in your wildest dreams! I know! Besides sheep, there's no other beast that can endure that weather!'

'Ah!' retorted *Wizard* with a winning smile. 'No cows in Norway, then?'

'Well... no, there shouldn't be,' said the sentry. 'Where is it exactly that Norway lies?'

'Well,' said *Wizard*, 'in any case, where they're going is not my business but the Agency's. My contract ends here, at the boat. Whatever happens from then on is not my thing. I deliver the animals and I'm off.'

He lit a cigarette.

'It is odd, though,' he said after a silence as he raised a boot to rest on the truck's fender. 'I knew I was late, but the Agency told me to come tonight anyway. They assured me that all the paperwork was in order and I would have no problems getting to the ship. Had I known better, I'd have waited until Monday, for as it is now I'll miss tomorrow's game! On the other hand, those on board will be stuck for another day here and that should be more complicated. Because as far as I know they were scheduled to sail tomorrow at first light, or at least that's why they asked me to come now anyway.'

'There's nothing I can do,' said the sentry, sitting down again on his stool.

For a while neither of them spoke. Suddenly the sentry asked, 'You don't happen to have any water in the cabin, do you?'

'Yes,' said *Wizard*. 'Is it for the *maté*?'

'Yes, for the *maté*. I emptied the thermos I had long ago and it's getting colder by the minute.'

Wizard opened the cabin door and climbed without closing it, looking for the thermos flask he always took on his trips.

'Do you have the paperwork?' asked the sentry from his stool, and added: 'Because if you don't there's no case, you'll have to wait until Monday and check through the new Customs building.' He raised an arm to indicate the direction. 'Over there, by the Maciel Gate.'

'No, no, of course I have them! That's already been fixed, look here!' *Wizard* climbed down from the cabin with the thermos in one hand and an envelope full of Customs forms in the other.

The sentry opened the envelope and read the papers with little attention.

'Excuse me,' he said while he examined them, 'any chance you could spare another cigarette? It's my wife, she takes them from my pockets as soon as she finds them and that's why I no longer buy them, but I can't quit the bloody things.'

'I have exactly the same problem,' said *Wizard*, taking the pack out once more as he searched for the lighter. 'Perhaps I've just learned to hide them better,' he ended with a short laugh.

'Yes,' said the sentry, reviewing the papers again before returning them to the envelope. 'Everything is in order and stamped. You could've got in if you'd arrived a little earlier. Are the seals still unbroken?'

'Of course they are!' said *Wizard*. 'The details are there on the manifest. There's nothing else. It's a pity to have the animals waiting on the truck for another day, don't you think? But it seems that they're fucked, so to speak. And the same goes for the boat. Unless, obviously,' he added lowering his voice, 'you give us a little hand here and we can get them through now, because I foresee that the Agency will blame me for arriving late.'

'I've already told you that I can't do anything!' insisted the sentry, throwing his arms open to signal his despair.

'You could open the gate and let me in.'

'No I can't. Well, actually I could. But it's against the rules.'

'So is smoking on your post. To say nothing about drinking *maté*.'

This time the sentry looked at him, narrowing his eyes.

'Two thousand,' he said tauntingly.

'Done!' said *Wizard*, taking out his wallet. 'One thousand now and the rest when I come out!' he added, handing the sentry half the money he had asked for.

'Okay!' said the sentry. 'But no headlights inside. And the whole thing will have to be quick.'

'No problem!' answered *Wizard*, climbing on the truck.

He led the lorry carefully between the shadows thrown by the stacks of containers scattered at the side of the freezing plant. He drove with the headlights off as requested, and in order to make sure everything was on schedule he took a mobile phone out of his pocket and dialled a number. It rang once before the call was answered and he recognised Eduardo's voice.

'Are you already here?'

'I'll be at the side in approximately two minutes.'

'I can see you already.' said Eduardo and terminated the call.

And Every Morning the Sun

When Eduardo returned to the shipyard everything was in good order. As he had predicted, during his absence the work continued without major obstacles. He was well aware that the secret to an efficient operation was in detailed planning and, before leaving, had spent many hours with his foremen carefully designing the tasks that each of the divisions would have to follow to maintain the rhythm of the current constructions. Now he verified with satisfaction that all the projects were on schedule.

His gig in *Rosamaría* had brought back the almost sensual pleasure of commanding a ship and he felt he had regained his optimism. He was once more in control of his life. Few things, if any, pleased him more than the intimate loneliness of a dark bridge as he sailed as master of a ship, way out at sea with nothing else to look at besides the stars and the restless, silvery waves. It was his version of standing duty on the stockades, watching over the slumber of others. This was the most intense way to feel alive. He knew he could deliver the same passion when required, and therefore looked forward to excelling in this new task.

He was pleased. 'I gave the Navy everything I had,' he said to himself, 'and nothing was given up as a sacrifice.' That was true. He had always liked what he was doing and, even though he had at times been in deep disagreement with his superiors, he had obeyed them for as long as he wore the Navy's uniform. That was what counted. That was his duty and his commitment, and fulfilling them was his measure of a man.

He would have welcomed more of it, but he knew life is too short to achieve everything. He liked to think that we always sail alone, but he also appreciated those unique moments that only friendship makes possible, such as that afternoon in Patrick's veranda when he read in the faces of his former comrades that they also thought the road – and therefore *his* road – had been worth it.

For once the afternoon was windless. Warming up like a cat in the sun, feeling at peace amid the extraordinary silence, Damián Lucena sat on a bench and enjoyed the stillness. Two days had elapsed since *Wizard* had returned, talking about things that made him remember the faces of the Malvinas. Or rather the eyes of the Malvinas, the blank stares on faces like ice, the sleepless hours.

He did not like to remember the war. He had buried the Islands along with their nightmares long ago. Now he was resting, his eyes closed and without any worry, in Sunday leisure. He felt the air cool around him and opened his eyes. Jorge Orcande's figure blocked the sun.

'And so?' asked Orcande. 'Did *Tata* come back with anything new?'

'Nothing new,' he answered. 'He came back a little tired, but it seems the trip was worth it. I guess it's always good to see old friends again, and here we're quite isolated.'

'Yes,' agreed Orcande. 'They were all Navy guys, right? From the Malvinas, I gathered.'

'Yes,' said Damián. 'It was the same group of divers that operated together in the Malvinas. Amazing that they all managed to get together again after so many years!'

Orcande sat down on the dirt, resting his back against the white wall. It burned to the touch after hours of sun-scorched heat. For a while none of them said a word until Lucena, his eyes still looking in front of him, said, 'It was all a long time ago.'

After a while Orcande got slowly to his feet, the great afternoon heat weighing visibly on his shoulders.

'I need to change a filter in the Bedford,' he said. 'Give me a hand?'

Damián Lucena stood up and followed him into the garage.